GRISWOLD'S OP

JOHN KOLOEN

WATCHFIRE
PRESS

GET THE NEWSLETTER

Visit watchfirepress.com/jk to subscribe to John Koloen's free author newsletter and receive exclusive news and discounts on John's upcoming novels.

ADAN BURKE'S ALOOFNESS CAME TO HIM NATURALLY, the product of his grandfather's anger during the long years the young man's father languished in prison, a victim of circumstances. He'd killed a man in a bar fight, hit him in the head with the fat end of a pool cue. The man had come at him during a game. He'd claimed Adan's father had moved the cue ball for a better lie. They were playing for money. Angry words were exchanged. It wasn't the first time his father had been accused of cheating, but it was the first time he'd killed someone.

The penalty for manslaughter in Texas is two to twenty years in state prison, and a fine not to exceed ten thousand dollars. Had it not been for his criminal record, he might have gotten the minimum, but because he had a previous assault, among lesser crimes, he got the maximum, leaving eight-year-old Adan in the care of Harley Burke, a broad-shouldered, gun-loving one-time member of the Ku Klux Klan. Adan's grandfather was livid over his son's incarceration, not because of his crime so much as how it would reflect on himself.

"When they pull up your name on the computer, they'll see mine—and some of your cousins. I guarantee it," the old man told him on his first and only visit to the Wallace Unit of the Texas Department of Criminal Justice in West Texas. "Hell, they pull me over for having a broken tail light they'll check me out twice hoping to find something to put me away for."

"What was I s'posed to do, Pops?" James Longstreet Burke—J.L. for short—contended. "He came at me."

"Yeah, with his fucking fists. I taught you to fight, didn't I?"

"You did, but I thought he had a pool ball in his hands and was gonna throw it or hit me in the head with it."

"But he didn't, did he?"

"No, sir, he didn't. But I'm payin' for it now."

"And so am I. I told you when you was growin' up about stayin' out of big time trouble, didn't I?"

"You did, but—"

"Don't but me," the old man interrupted angrily. "Besides that, you pissed off the judge and he put you out here in the middle of goddamn nowhere. You know how long it took me to drive here?"

J.L., dressed in prison orange, shrugged.

"Nine and one-half fucking hours. And then I got here too late for visiting hours and had to spend a night in a motel so I could see you today."

"I'm glad you did, Pops," J. L. said, struggling to ignore his father's anger. "It hasn't been a picnic for me, either. And can you keep it down? They'll throw you out. They don't put up with shit here."

"Fuck you and your picnic. And fuck them. I don't have enough money for another motel so I'm either gonna drive through the night or I'll pull over somewhere and hope the cops don't put a light on me. That's all I need with this little snot-nose with me."

Adan watched warily as his grandfather and father sparred. Other than nodding at him when they sat down in the visitor's room, his father had said little to the youngster. J.L. was living at his father's place when Adan was born, the result of a fling with a woman he barely knew but who moved in with him and Harley when she learned she was pregnant. It was too late in the pregnancy for J.L. to talk her into an abortion. Besides, Harley wanted to see if the child was a boy. He'd told his son that either way, the woman was going to leave after the pregnancy, but he told J.L. to keep the baby if it was a boy.

Adan didn't know the details of his birth, had no memory of his mother. Didn't even know her name. All he knew for certain was that she was white and had had sex with his father, who refused to respond to any of his questions about her. Even so, he loved his father and wanted J.L. to love him. He'd hoped after the first visit he'd have other chances to see him but his grandfather didn't see it the same way.

After they'd returned to Vidor, Harley poured beer into a shot glass and handed it to the eight-year-old.

"You're my son, now," he said, gruffly. "Drink up."

HARLEY FLEW AN AMERICAN FLAG IN HIS FRONT YARD, with a Confederate Navy Jack underneath it. Situated on an unimproved rural road outside of Vidor, the property abutted the edge of a pine forest. It stood in a small cluster of mid-century tract houses, most vacant and overgrown with shoulder-height weeds. With few residents, the neighborhood was quiet, which is just the way Harley liked it, except when he wanted to make noise. Now and then he would squeeze off a few rounds from one of his ten rifles and half-dozen handguns, often aiming at feral cats, squirrels and other varmints. The cat carcasses he threw into the weeds of an adjacent house. The squirrels he would eat. Nobody complained.

Having quit school during the seventh grade, Harley had little use for education. The only book in the house was a lightly read Bible. However, the old man knew that if Adan didn't attend school the authorities would sooner or later come knocking on his dilapidated door, so during the school year he made sure Adan was in class, even if he was sick.

Harley hated authorities just as much as he hated minorities. He hated the way they dressed, the way they talked, the contempt that poured out of them like sweat. He knew they didn't like him, but he was smart enough to keep a low profile. It wasn't that he was a criminal. He had a misdemeanor record but, aside from a few days in county lockup, he'd never served a sentence.

"They treat me like that because I'm...whatyoumacallit, unconventional," he told Adan one evening after polishing off his fifth beer. "They don't like that I don't shave. They don't like that I don't work for a living. They're jealous. You know, I been an outsider all my life. But as long as I got my guns there's nothing they can do about it."

It's like he told his son when he was growing up.

"Don't get in over your head," Harley told him. "When things go to hell, you run. Don't look back. Don't feel like you gotta stick with your buddies. They just ain't smart enough to run. You know, sometimes a young fella thinks he's Superman and does something stupid that puts him away. I'm here to tell you, you're no Superman and the best thing that can happen to you is that you don't get caught."

Like his father, Adan didn't like school. But back in the day, Harley thought, if a student dropped out, nobody cared. The authorities didn't come looking for him like they do now. It was easier back then. Harley didn't care so why should the authorities care? he reasoned. They were his spawn. The authorities didn't put a roof over their heads. The authorities didn't feed them. Take that back: The kids received free school lunches on account of Harley's limited declared income. That was one good thing the authorities did. But everything else they did, he could just as well do without.

And the disability he received, he earned it, breaking a

hip while roughnecking. He couldn't work after that. Couldn't stand up for long periods, or walk without pain for that matter. Sitting was fine.

But it wasn't as if Harley didn't educate his grandson. He tried to teach him how to box, but the boy was small and skinny and couldn't take a jab to the head, unlike his father who stood up to his father like a punching bag. J.L. looked like his father, stocky and several inches taller at just under six feet. J.L. was still muscular, but the old man had spent too many years avoiding work. What with his beer drinking and lack of regular activity, his muscle had settled across his belly like a soccer ball. Harley figured the boy took after his mother. He was wiry and small like her. He had her grey eyes and dark hair, which he wore long.

Harley's house was set back from the road, shaded by several southern yellow pines. The roof was patched with tarps and leaked during thunderstorms. The living room was furnished with a single rocking chair, a dark brown loveseat that looked like it had been abandoned on the side of a road, and a forty-two inch flat screen TV that he'd purchased at a thrift store along with an end table to support the TV. He also had a Lifeline land line that he used for outgoing calls but otherwise kept unplugged to avoid telemarketers. One of the walls was festooned with a large Confederate battle flag in pristine condition. Overhead, a 52-inch ceiling fan wobbled like a poorly thrown Frisbee whenever it was turned on. A wicker hamper filled with empty beer bottles and cans stood in a corner next to a large gun cabinet. An ancient air-conditioner pumped coolish air into the room from a side window. The wall-to-wall carpeting was threadbare and scabrous.

The two bedrooms were in similar condition, each lit by a bare bulb dangling from the ceiling with its patchy mildew. The bathroom and kitchen sinks drained slowly and flies seemed to have proprietary rights on the kitchen. The sink was always full of dirty dishes, the two washing only what they needed when they needed it. Harley's saving grace was that he owned the property outright and all he had to do to keep it was to pay his taxes, which he did, always at the last minute at the tax office in Vidor. It was the only expense that he could not avoid, as he carried no insurance. But it was his property, located in an unincorporated area where no one could tell him how to live, not even the authorities.

Freedom was big with Harley. As was the superiority of the white race, the race that had made the modern world possible—or so he told Adan, who had learned never to argue with his grandfather. The old man kept a leather strap on a hook in the bathroom and he was not averse to use it.

Vidor, population about eleven thousand, was the perfect community for an unreconstructed racist. Residents claiming Hawaiian ethnicity outnumbered blacks nineteen to thirteen. Adan rarely saw black people but he read about them on the internet and watched them on TV, which mostly showed them doing bad things.

"I used this on your father," he told Adan during one beating after the youngster told him about being bullied at school. "It toughed him up. Made him hard. No son of mine is going to grow up a sissy. You go back and take care of that bully."

"But I can't," the then eleven-year-old cried as the strap landed across his legs. "They're bigger than me."

"Then use your fucking head," Harley shouted and suddenly stopped spanking the boy. "What did I tell you about running?"

"You said it's better to run than get caught."

"I would never tell your dad to run from a bully, but you're a runt."

"They can run, too," he whined.

The next day Harley started the boxing instruction, but the boy was small and the old man was big and he was drunk. The more that Adan flailed, his short arms unable to land a blow, the more Harley taunted him, the more aggressive he became, angry at the boy's weakness, daring him to grow into a man right in front of him. Harley quit trying after he gave his grandson a black eye and grew fearful that a teacher at the school would notice and the authorities would barge in on his world. He kept him from school the next day and the lessons ceased. Adan never complained to his grandfather about being bullied again.

3

ADAN HAD ONE GOAL WHEN HE TURNED FIFTEEN AND A half: get a learner's permit to drive. The old man balked at paying one hundred thirty dollars for the approved driver's course offered by the school district.

"You know how I learned to drive," Harley told his grandson, now a full five-feet six inches tall and one hundred twenty pounds. "I got into my older brother's Nash and drove up and down all the back roads in the county. Didn't have no driving school. And I've never had an accident that was my fault. Never. Hell, for a long time I didn't even have a license."

Adan knew better than to ask his grandfather to pay for the driver's course, but for twenty dollars he could register for the parent-taught program through the Department of Public Safety.

"No way we're going to a DPS office," Harley said emphatically. "No way."

"We can do it online," Adan said hopefully.

"And how we gonna do that? We don't got no online."

"I can do it at school. Or we can mail it in. Please. I don't ask for much."

"Maybe if you had a job you could pay for it yourself."

Adan sighed. Living in the boondocks without transportation put him at a disadvantage when it came to employment. He rode a bus to and from school but getting around on his own always meant walking. Lots of walking. For his thirteenth birthday Adan's grandfather had given him a bicycle that he bought at a thrift store, but the roads near his house were poorly maintained and the bike itself was too small, resulting in sore knees. He didn't complain, though, and his grandfather never noticed that the boy didn't ride the bike. It was that way with most of the gifts his grandfather bought. He asked for a backpack to carry books and what he got was a polyester pack meant for elementary students emblazoned with kittens. He thanked his grandfather and never used it, preferring a discarded canvas tote bag he'd found at school.

Frustrated, he thought about what he could do to make twenty dollars. A job was out of the question. Shoplifting came to mind. He'd done it before and hadn't been caught. But what could he steal that he could sell for twenty dollars? There was no point asking any of his few friends. None of them had any money they could lend. His grandfather had already turned him down and now the old man had fallen into a stuporous nap in his rocking chair. He knew his grandfather kept cash in a coffee can in the kitchen but Adan was too afraid of him to even touch it. Harley had made it clear that the can was his, what was inside it was his and it was nobody else's business. It was so unfair. Even his friends had cell phones. And many of the kids at school had smartphones, fashionable clothing and cars.

"Why can't I have anything, goddamnit?" he said aloud, staring at the cabinet containing the coffee can. He approached it like a predator sneaking up on its prey, silently pulling the cabinet door, revealing the can in a corner.

A noise came from the living room, freezing him where he stood. His head shivered. Instantly, he did an about face and moving toward the doorway, peeked into the living room. He listened to his grandfather's labored breathing. He listened to the ceiling fan. He watched until he was satisfied the old man was still asleep. Stepping lightly toward the cabinet he grabbed the can and set it on the orange Formica counter, his mind racing, calculating whether the risk was worth the reward. He knew his grandfather to be a shrewd and vindictive man who would not hesitate to punish him. Since his boxing lessons the old man had limited his physical contact to slaps and pinches that didn't leave marks. But that was when he was under control. He was also capable of rage, and that was what Adan feared, the old man losing control and taking it out on him.

It hadn't occurred to him that even if he had the twenty dollars, he'd have to forge his grandfather's signature on the DPS form. It hadn't occurred to him that registering online required a credit card, which his grandfather didn't have. Maybe he should have talked to Harley about the benefits if he had a license. He could run errands. Maybe he could get a job and repay the old man. But there was no way he could say anything that sounded as if he wasn't contradicting the old man. That's another thing that would set him off. Adan wasn't thinking about the requirements for a teen to get a license. About the paperwork and the complicated procedures and the forty-four hours of behind the wheel instruction. But it didn't matter because Adan wasn't thinking that far ahead. All he was focused on was getting the twenty dollars.

With one last glance at his snoring grandfather, the teen lifted the plastic lid and stared at two wads of bills, one stacked on top of the other, each nearly the diameter of the can.

We're rich! he screamed in his head as he nervously brushed his fingers across the currency, sniffing it. The money smelled like coffee.

Squeezing his fingers into the can, he pulled out the top wad, held together by a thick rubber band, surprised by its heft and weight. He couldn't remember the last time he'd been this excited. It was more money than he'd ever imagined. But it wasn't his and he knew that and suddenly grew fearful. He couldn't shake the feeling that he was being watched. He couldn't stop himself from looking over his shoulder and then, after removing the rubber band, peeling off two twenties and stuffing them into his pants pocket. Replacing the rubber band, he struggled to get the wad to fit into the can. Removing the band had allowed the wad to loosen. Panic started to set in. He removed the rubber band again and, squeezing the wad, replaced the band and managed to push it into the can, barely. Replacing the plastic lid, he returned the can to the cabinet and, filled with excitement and fear, hurried out the back door, closing it silently behind him, as he entered the backyard jumping for joy.

4

LIKE ANY YOUNG MAN WITH A FORTY DOLLAR WINDFALL
on a sunny Saturday afternoon, Adan wanted to show off.
He also didn't want to wake his grandfather so he didn't
dare use the landline to call his best friend Jason Whitman.
Instead, energized by his newfound wealth, he trotted into
town, hoping Jason would be home. Jason was also a high
school outcast. He lived with his mother, who worked two
jobs—one as a waitress and the other walking the floors at
Wal-Mart. The two-bedroom shotgun house with detached-
garage was in a working class neighborhood of smallish
houses. Laboring fifty hours a week, his mother was seldom
home and when she was she was often asleep, either recov-
ering from or resting for her next shift. Her latchkey son was
accustomed to getting by on his own, fixing his own meals
and helping his mother by washing dishes, mowing the lawn
and other things a responsible man would do for his wife.

"Hey, Whit," Adan said as Jason responded to the
knocking on the back door. "Is your mom home?"

"Hey, man. Nope. She's at work. What up?" he said as
he made way for Adan to enter the house. From the narrow

back entry, they stepped up into the small, brightly painted kitchen, which, like the rest of the house, was immaculate. The boys took seats at a table in the cramped dinette, painted yellow like the kitchen.

"You know, I really like your house," Adan said, nodding approvingly. "Everything's so clean."

"I know, I know. You say that all the time," Jason said, eyeing Adan expectantly. "So, what's up?"

Smiling, Adan pulled out the crumpled twenties from his pocket, setting them on the table between them.

"Wow! Where'd you get that?"

"From my gramps."

"Oh, yeah, right. Like he'd give you anything."

"No, really."

"I don't believe it. Where'd you get it, really? You didn't grab it out of a cash register somewhere, did you?"

"No, nothing like that. I took it from his stash. He's loaded."

Jason looked at his friend with amazement.

"You stole money from your grandpa?"

"Well, yeah, you could say that," Adan said. "But there's a whole lot more where this came from. Two big wads the size of a coffee can. I couldn't believe it."

"You don't think he's not gonna miss it? I mean, whenever I think of your grandfather I think of the giant in *Jack in the Beanstalk*. He's a mean dude, man. He even punched you out, right?"

"Aw, he was just teachin' me to box."

"Yeah, teaching you to be a punching bag."

"OK, OK. He's an asshole, what can I say? But he's loaded."

Jason was six months older than Adan, taller and more filled out. He already had his learner's permit and planned to take the official driver's instruction course as soon as his mother could pay for it. He had already gotten to the point that she let him drive her on errands in town, but not on the highway. His mother wasn't in a rush because she knew she could never afford his insurance. She'd been encouraging him to apply for part-time jobs, but he had yet to see the urgency.

"So what do you want to do?" Jason asked.

"Does your mom have the car?"

"Yep. She's at work."

"I was thinking we could go to Beaumont, maybe go to a bowling alley or shoot some pool, but we'd need a car."

Jason shook his head.

"There's just nothing to do in this shitty town," Adan lamented. "I was hoping we could do something."

"I know what you're thinking but I'm not gonna steal my mom's car. I can't afford to get caught. Not that you can but, fuck."

Adan slumped in his chair and started rapping the table with his knuckles.

"I know. We could go to Conn Park. Go swimming. Maybe meet some girls," Jason said optimistically.

"That's so lame. I don't have a swim suit. Besides, I can't swim."

"I got an extra one," Jason said.

"You're bigger than me."

"It'll fit you. Besides, we might meet some girls."

"It's like five bucks apiece, right?"

"Yeah, something like that. Anyway, I can pay my own way ...."

"Nope," Adan said emphatically, picking up the twenties and waving them. "This is on me."

Having pilfered once and gotten away with it, Adan was encouraged to do it again. And again. At the same time, after several hours on a computer in the school library, he finally recognized the impossibility of getting a driver's license. He discovered that he couldn't forge the paperwork for a learner's permit, as the state required him to appear at a driver's license office with his parent or guardian. And before he could apply for the permit he'd have to complete a teen driver's education course that included behind the wheel training, which cost four hundred dollars. He feared his grandfather would hit him if he even asked for such an extravagant amount. And there was no way he could steal it. The more he learned, the emptier he felt. It was worse than being punched in the stomach. It was made worse because all around him he saw other kids getting their learner's permits and licenses, achieving a dream that for him was out of reach.

At seventeen and starting his senior year, his grades had slipped along with his interest in school. Tired of being skinny, during the summer break he started a body building program in his backyard. At first, he did curls with buckets of soil until his arms ached and then, with the money he'd been pilfering from the coffee can, he'd acquired a used barbell set and a prepaid cell phone. He told Harley a friend had given the weights to him. He didn't tell him about the cell phone. At school, he learned as much as he could about weight training and lamented that he couldn't afford supplements but felt he was on thin ice where the coffee can was concerned. Even though he'd put on several pounds of muscle, it wasn't enough to keep the bullies from picking on him. However, it was enough to make him feel that he didn't have to run without first taking a shot. If he could land one good punch, hit his tormenters before they hit him, he'd send a message that he was no longer the skinny weakling.

But he was wrong.

The bullies taunted him. He lashed out. Landed several punches. And then they beat the shit out of him.

HARLEY TOOK ONE LOOK AT HIS BEATEN AND BLOODIED grandson, sprang from his chair and flew into a rage, grabbing an empty beer bottle and throwing it on the floor, shattering it, glass shards flying across the room.

"Who did this to you?" he demanded, his face contorted, eyes glaring, nose-flaring.

"The same guys."

"They've gone too far this time. We're going back to that school and ...."

He stopped in mid-sentence.

"And do what? Talk to the principal? The school knows about these guys. I'm not the only one they pick on."

Harley went into the kitchen, pulled a beer out of the refrigerator and then slumped into his chair in the living room. Angrily twisting the cap off, he drained a third of it in a single gulp and wiped his hairy hand across his hairy face. He hated the whole damn thing. He hated the authorities for not protecting Adan and he hated Adan for not protecting himself. Most of all he hated himself for not doing something. Had this happened on the street somewhere he'd be out there with his guns. He wouldn't back down. He'd find the suckers and let Smith and Wesson put the fear of God in them. But it happened in the light of day, in a place where they'd sit him down in a room and talk to him like he was a child and try to calm him down, seeing him as more of a threat than the bullies who, protected by well-off parents and cooperative authorities, were, after all, picking on kids who didn't fit in.

Adan knew that his grandfather hated snitches. It's one of the things he'd told J.L. before they locked him up in West Texas.

"Don't go around snitching on nobody, no matter what. Snitches don't live long," he'd told him on that day he visited him. But J.L. knew this. His old man had been telling him this all his life. And Adan knew that his grandfather wasn't going to do anything to the bullies. Not unless they attacked him. And even though everyone in school knew his dad was in prison for manslaughter, they'd never seen Harley and he wanted to keep it that way. Keeping Harley inconspicuous was a priority. That's why when Harley let him drive the 1982 Ford pickup with its rusty hood and mismatched fenders on county roads even though he didn't have a learner's permit Adan didn't want to do it. Thought it would screw things up if they were stopped, but then he wanted to drive so much that he decided it didn't matter.

"Goddamnit, boy, I'm gonna teach you to drive whether you got a license or not," he'd blustered that first time. But he had little patience for the gear-grinding, the stops and starts as Adan tried to figure out the clutch.

"Just let it up," the old man bellowed, "what the fuck is so hard about that?"

Concentrating on the clutch, staring at the floor shifter,

Adan caused the truck to lurch backward across the road in front of their house and into a drainage ditch, earning a hard slap on the back of his head as if he'd done it on purpose.

Adan practiced coordinating the clutch and shifter on his own until he could do it without looking down. Then it got easier. He'd drive his grandfather on every back road in Orange County, avoiding populated areas and the authorities. Driving seemed natural to Adan, and he enjoyed it. He enjoyed driving with the window down and his arm on the door, feeling the wind across his face, with only the slightest uneasiness that all it would take to ruin it was the sight of a cop in the rearview mirror. Anytime he saw a vehicle in the mirror, no matter how far away, he felt uneasy, watching the mirror until the vehicle turned off or got close enough that he could relax because it wasn't a cop. He didn't worry about his grandfather when the old man was at home. Nothing bad would happen to him there. But on the road, if they got stopped, he had no idea what would happen, what his grandfather would be charged with and then, what would happen to him with no guardian. The authorities had already taken away his father and, even though deep down he was afraid of his grandfather, he was all that was left of his family.

That's why he didn't want his grandfather to get involved with the bullies. It wasn't because he didn't want anything to be done about it. It was because even though he was afraid of him, he needed him and would protect him from himself if it came to that. Searing with the humiliation and pain of the beating on that long walk home, he knew what he was going to do about it even before his grandfather threw his beer bottle. He was going to show them that even though they were bigger and outnumbered him and wouldn't be held accountable because of their families' stature in the community, he wasn't going to allow them to get away with it. He had a plan.

7

"You're crazy," Jason told Adan as they stood outside the high school near the football practice field Friday morning. "Anyway, I don't believe you."

Adan smiled, touching his book bag, which hung heavily from his shoulder. No one paid attention to them as students milled about prior to the start of classes.

"Promise you won't tell," Adan said slyly, looking around nervously.

"Promise I won't tell what?"

"Just promise," Adan coaxed, rearranging the bag so that Jason could see inside.

"What the fuck!" Jason exclaimed.

"Quiet," Adan said quickly, stamping his feet slightly. "Not so loud."

Jason shook his head.

"I can't believe you're doing this. You're a senior for chrissake. You'll graduate in the spring."

"That's why I'm doing it. I'm tired of it. They shouldn't be picking on seniors like this."

"They pick on me, too," Jason whined.

"Yeah, but they don't beat the shit outta you."

"Well, I don't fight back. Your problem is you try to fight back. It wasn't so bad before the last time, you know."

The two stood in silence for a moment.

"Is it loaded?"

"Are you kidding? No, it's not loaded. I wouldn't bring a loaded gun to school."

Jason sighed.

"Still, you could get expelled or go to jail. Your grandpa could go to jail, did you think about that?"

"I thought you were my friend."

"I am your friend," Jason protested. "I'm your best friend. Hell, I'm your only friend. But this, I don't know, Adan."

"I'm just gonna scare 'em, that's all."

"Man, you're scaring me," Jason said as the bell rang and they parted ways.

8

Adan didn't have a plan per se. He thought he'd wait to see how things developed. If the bullies didn't come around, then he wouldn't go looking for them. This wasn't the first time he'd thought about bringing a gun to school. He wasn't stupid. He knew how much trouble he could get into. He also knew it was getting worse. The last time he tried to stand his ground the way his grandfather said he should hadn't worked out.

"Always take out the leader or the biggest guy first," Harley had told him, more than once. "Just punch him straight on the bridge of the nose as hard as you can, or across the throat. The rest of them will run, more than likely."

No, it hadn't worked out that way. Adan landed a few punches, but nowhere near the head. And there were three of them, all of them bigger than him. He'd tried to run after it became obvious that he couldn't put up a fight the way his grandfather had told him. All he could do in the end was curl up into a ball and try to minimize the damage as they finished their work by kicking him while he was down. He didn't want to tell his grandfather how he'd ended up in a ball on the ground so he embellished, made it sound like a straight up fight until the numbers worked against him. He told Harley he'd done what he told him to do but missed. That was another thing Harley had mentioned. Don't miss.

"You only get one shot in a fight to end it quickly," Harley had said, dredging up a story of how he'd won fights that he otherwise would've lost had he not struck first. But looking at the skinny boy, he shook his head.

"'Course, it wouldn't hurt if you put on twenty pounds, bulked up, you know. I seen you lifting weights out back. That's good. But it don't happen overnight."

Harley's incipient racism had little outlet in a town that was almost entirely white. Nobody seemed offended by his Confederate Navy Jack. But over time he began to hate on people of his own race, liberals who wanted nonwhites to move into the moribund town and, he believed, looked down on people like him. He saw it at the grocery store all the time. He could see it in the way they averted their eyes when he walked by, the way they looked down, the way they looked away as if a shelf lined with cereal boxes suddenly became more important than him. Sure, he didn't bathe and his coveralls were dirty and his beard was unruly and he scowled like he was mad at the world, and he had a reputation, but he knew when the race wars came these fine white citizens would welcome him into their arms, a fighter with experience from way back when Vidor had gained its reputation as the most racist town in Texas.

But not even he would put it into his grandson's head to bring a gun to school.

By the end of his second period class, Adan's mood had moved on. Several students who had heard about the fight asked how he did and when he told them that he'd stood up against Joshua Dearborn, several gave him thumbs up. He was not the only target, which somehow made him feel better about getting beat up. And then there they were, the three of them, blocking his way between buildings on his way to the cafeteria, his heavy book bag slung over his shoulder. Alone.

He knew the drill. They'd try to dump his bag on the ground. Call him names. Ask him how it felt to go home to his drunken grandfather every night, and about his father languishing in prison. What a family, they'd say. A bunch of criminals lowering the collective IQ of the community. Too stupid to get out of their own way and the stupid seventeen-year-old who carried books because he couldn't afford a laptop or even a pad.

"So, how's your dad doing?" Dearborn, the leader, sneered. "I hear he gets along real well with all the men."

They had made a living insulting his family. Everyone in town knew about his dad and his grandfather. Newspapers covered his dad's arrest and trial. And Adan thought he had gotten beyond it. Had learned to ignore the insults. But there was that deep sense of unfair treatment that somehow had survived every attempt to destroy it. He knew his father's story and how he was only defending himself and how unfair the judge and prosecutor had been and how lame the defense attorney was. He knew his grandfather's story, some of which appalled him and some of which was his own story. Unlike his grandfather, Adan didn't know whether he hated blacks.

This time though, as Dearborn encroached on his personal space, he reached into the bag, knowing exactly where the gun was, and pulled it out, raising it slowly like he did during target practice, steadying it with both hands, pointing it at the leader. Contrary to what he expected, this only caused them to ridicule him.

"You putz," Dearborn taunted. "You think we're afraid of you? I can see from here you don't have a clip. It's a fucking nine mil and it ain't got a clip. You must think we're fools."

But then an unexpected thing happened as they lurched toward him. Adan squeezed the trigger and the gun went bang and the leader's expression turned from contempt to utter surprise as his right shoulder reacted to the impact of the bullet from the clipless gun.

For a moment the four of them froze. And then the leader screamed, falling to the ground while his companions stared at Adan, fear contorting their faces even as Adan struggled to understand what had happened.

But like a jack rabbit with a book bag, he turned and ran, his mind outracing his legs, trying to understand what had happened when shooting someone was the furthest thing from his mind. He had left the clip at home to avoid such a thing and here it had happened anyway. And by the time he'd reached his house, out of breath, his legs aching, it was clear that there was a round in the chamber, that he had forgotten to do the only thing his grandfather always told him to do with a nine millimeter, never leave a round in the chamber.

ADAN HAD ONLY ONE THING IN MIND, ESCAPING. Tiptoeing through the backdoor, he saw his grandfather snoring in his chair in the living room, the ceiling fan spinning at a precarious speed. Grabbing the duffel bag he used to take dirty clothes to the laundromat, he stuffed it with as many of his belongings as would fit, mostly clothing, including his heavy sweater, his poncho and blanket. He thought about taking his pillow but it took up too much space. He had yet to formulate a destination but he knew he couldn't stay in Vidor and he didn't want to be home when the police came knocking. At the same time, he didn't want to jam up the old man so he left a note on the kitchen table explaining what had happened, how it was a mistake and that he was only trying to scare the bullies. He grabbed his grandfather's flashlight and a kitchen knife and utensils and stuffed them into the duffel. If only he had more time. He knew he would need more things but couldn't settle himself enough to think logically.

Pausing momentarily as if to catch his breath, his eyes came to rest on the cabinet with his grandfather's money.

He had only a few dollars. There was no question he'd need more. What would his grandfather think about him taking his money? It was a transitory thought, one of many piling up in his head all at once. But the other thoughts, such as how he would get out of town, where he would go, all of them, evaporated like a distant memory as he quietly opened the cabinet, pulling out the can. He hesitated slightly after popping the lid. But there was no choice. If he expected to get away, he'd have to commit another crime, this one against his own flesh and blood. He pulled the upper wad of currency and set it on the table where it expanded against the rubber band that held it. He replaced the can carefully, as if he had taken only one of two bills as usual and returned the rest. His grandfather would know as soon as he saw the note that he'd also been robbed. He'd know it without even looking.

"I'm sorry I took the money," Adan added to his note. "I'll pay you back. I promise."

He signed it *Adan Burke*.

He put several twenties into his wallet, which held his student ID, and stuffed the rest into a plastic bag, tying the ends together before stuffing it into the center of the duffel, zipping it and quietly slipping out the back door like the thief he was.

HE KNEW HE COULDN'T HITCHHIKE OUT OF TOWN.
Shooting a student would have brought out the entire police
force, even the sheriff's department. Someone would see
him lugging the duffel bag. It would look odd. The authorities would be called. There would be no escape.

Which is why instead of walking toward Vidor, he
walked away from it, into Orange County, down back roads
he'd driven with his grandfather, only not on the road,
alongside it, in the brush, behind trees, concealing himself
as best he could, dropping to the ground when he saw a car
in the distance. It happened only twice but each time his
heart raced and he trembled with fear. Finally, as the sun
faded and darkness started to settle over the landscape, he
found a place under a stand of pine trees, away from the
road. Gathering pine branches for a mattress, he spread his
blanket and for the first time in what seemed forever, he lay
down, staring through the tree tops, listening for voices, for
cars, for footsteps in the underbrush.

Even though he was exhausted, sleep was out of the
question. His mind still raced, only instead of wondering

where he would go and how he would get there, he thought of the things he didn't have, such as food and water and mosquito repellent. With no wind, the insects filled the air with their incessant buzzing, forcing him to cover himself with the blanket in defense. No sooner had the mosquitoes become a nonissue than the second-guessing began. Should he have taken his grandfather's truck? How much farther could he have gotten? With a truck, he could have driven into the parking lot of a rural convenience store and bought all the food, water and mosquito repellant he needed and nobody would ask a question. But if he walked up carrying a duffel bag, they'd be suspicious. He'd be suspicious of such a person. He'd be out of place. It would invite scrutiny. Maybe a phone call.

But he couldn't imagine doing that to his grandfather. Taking his truck would be worse than taking half his money. It wasn't like he could take half his truck. Besides, it was an old truck. It could break down at any time. Maybe he couldn't even have gotten it to start but the noise of trying might have awakened his grandfather, who would have charged out the door like a bear with a bad hip. What would have happened then? Would the old man have helped him escape, or turn on him? He didn't know.

But it was pointless to think about such things. He needed a plan, somehow to get out of Orange County, out of Texas to some place where they wouldn't be looking for a teenager who'd shot a fellow student. He was grateful that the bullet had hit the bully in the shoulder and not the chest. Not knowing that it was loaded, he'd aimed the gun but without the heedfulness he used when shooting at targets when he expected and wanted to hit a bullseye. He could just as easily have killed the boy. And then what?

If only he could catch a ride. Get on a bus. But how

could he do that lying there in the dark woods, hiding from mosquitoes? He pulled out his twenty dollar Alcatel and scrolled through the few names on his contact list. Reception was stronger than he'd expected. According to the phone, it was nearly nine thirty. He wondered whether it was too late to call someone.

11

Harley Burke was awake when several police cars came to a stop in clouds of dust in front of his house. Four beefy guys in uniforms, guns drawn, were at the screen door before the old man could even get out of his chair. Behind them were two men in white shirts and ties, their eyes hidden behind dark glasses. One of them pulled a folded paper from the inside pocket of his tan sport jacket.

"Harley Burke, we have a warrant to search the premises. Please come to the door with your hands where we can see them."

"That means now," one of the uniformed officers barked.

Harley struggled to lift himself out of his chair and then fell back into it as the officers stormed into the room, nearly ripping the screen door from its hinges.

"What a dump," he heard one of them say as they searched each room, guns drawn. Satisfied that Adan wasn't there, they surrounded the old man, who looked up at them with a mixture of fear and contempt.

"What the fuck do you think you're doing?" he protested loudly.

"Your son, Adan, he shot someone at school."

"That's bullshit. Adan's my grandson. He wouldn't do that."

"Oh, no," one of the detectives said. "We have witnesses that saw him do it."

While the old man tried to figure out what was going on, two of the uniforms pointed toward a large cabinet with a glass front that was filled with rifles and shotguns. Below it they found his handgun collection in a drawer that ran the width of the cabinet.

"That's quite an arsenal you got there," the detective said, after examining the cache. "Is that where your grandson got the gun he used?"

"I don't know what the fuck you're talking about," Harley argued.

"How many handguns do you own, sir?" the second detective asked.

"A half dozen, six. Why?"

The detectives conferred.

"I count five," the first detective said. "Can you account for the sixth one, which seems to be missing?"

Harley tried to rise out of his chair but one of the detectives told him to remain seated.

"Well, how do I know what gun is missing if I can't look at them? I'm trying to cooperate here."

The detectives exchanged glances and escorted the old man to the cabinet.

"It's a nine mil. I can't believe he took it. He usually shoots a revolver."

One of the uniforms summoned the first detective to the kitchen while the second detective questioned Harley about his grandson. One of the uniforms reported that there was little clothing in Adan's bedroom.

"Look at this note," the uniform said to the first detective. "Says he didn't know the gun was loaded."

"Yeah, well, it's probably a lie. Bag it."

"What are they doing in my kitchen?" Harley demanded.

"They're executing the warrant, sir."

"What're they looking for?"

"Evidence."

"Hey, Tom," the first detective shouted. "You need to see this."

Leaving Harley in the custody of one of the uniforms, Tom approached the kitchen. On the table was a coffee can, which the first detective emptied onto the table.

"Will you look at that?" he said, nodding toward the large wad of currency. "I found it in a cabinet."

"What the fuck?"

"Yeah, where does white trash like him get a pile like that?"

Over the next hour Harley watched as the police placed his weapons and ammunition into evidence bags, followed by items removed from Adan's room. Photos were taken and one of the officers lifted fingerprints in Adan's room. Harley fumed but recognized the helplessness of his situation. Despite what the police told him, he didn't believe Adan would take a gun to school, much less shoot someone.

"If your grandson calls or somehow you're in touch with him, you might encourage him to turn himself in. It'll be better for him and everyone involved. We want this to end peacefully but because he used a gun in the commission of a crime he's considered to be armed and dangerous."

"What about my stuff? Where you taking it? Those

guns don't belong to Adan. They're mine and I have a right to have them."

"Read the warrant, sir," Tom said coldly. "It says we're authorized to confiscate weapons and other items that may have been used in the commission of a crime."

"You guys, you got it all working for you, don'tcha," Harley ranted. "You take people's guns and you leave them defenseless."

Ignoring the old man, the police finished their business. As they returned to their vehicles, Tom thanked Harley for his cooperation.

"Don't I get a receipt or something for the stuff you took?"

"You can request one at the station."

"So, you can just take my stuff and for all I know keep it for yourselves since I got no proof what you took. Is that it?"

"Sir, we executed a search warrant for a suspect involved in a shooting. Thanks for your cooperation."

Harley leaned against the front door jamb and watched as the cars drove away, his anger rising rapidly as if it had popped a cork. Letting loose a flurry of shouts and screams he went to his gun cabinet and pounded the wall. The guns were the most valuable possessions he owned. Sometimes he'd sell one when he needed money and replace it when things were flush. And then it occurred to him that he had something else of value. Nearly tripping over a rent in the living room carpet, he made a beeline for the kitchen.

Staring at the table in disbelief, he threw the empty coffee can across the room and screamed like a wounded animal.

Jason Whitman was quick to respond to Adan's text, even though he was supposed to be in bed.

Where R U? Whitman responded.

Cn I call U now? Adan texted.

Jason, who was at his desk in his bedroom, the door closed, stared at his phone. Word of the shooting went viral almost from the instant it had happened. The Beaumont TV stations led the local evening news with it. No names were mentioned but everyone at school knew who had been involved. It would only be a matter of time before Adan's class photo would become locally infamous, or famous, depending on whether one was a victim of the bullies. Already, Jason wondered whether the police would question him. People at school knew they were friends. Already he regretted responding to Adan's text.

Call me, Jason texted, switched off his phone's ringer and waited for it to vibrate.

"Whutsup, dude?" Jason said as if beginning a normal conversation.

"I didn't mean to shoot him," Adan said apologetically.

In a breathless moment, Adan explained what had happened, how it had happened and how fucked he was as a result.

"I'm seventeen. They'll try me as an adult. I'll end up in prison like my dad, just like those assholes at school said I would. Just like my gramps said I would."

"He told you that?"

"When he was drunk, which is like all the time."

"Are you gonna turn yourself in?"

"You think that's what I should do?"

"I don't know. You didn't kill him or anything like that. I couldn't believe it when I heard about it."

"What'd you think?"

"I thought, what the fuck."

"But you thought I did it?"

"Well, people said you did so, yeah, how could I not believe it? And then on the news, whoa. But they didn't name you."

"And they didn't show my pitcher?"

"Nothing. They didn't even say who got shot, just that he was in the hospital in Beaumont with non-life threatening injuries."

Adan sighed. He hadn't given any thought to turning himself in, but now he wondered whether that was better than running.

"My dad didn't run and look what it got him."

"Yeah."

"What did your mom say?"

"The usual mom stuff. She said I should stay away from you."

"What'd you say?"

"I'm talking to you, aren't I? What difference does it

make what I told her? I tell her stuff all the time that I know she wants to hear."

"So, you told her what? About me?"

"I said you got bullied a lot, more than everybody, really, except maybe Billy Baxter. He thought what you did was dope. He said they had it coming and he wished you'd shot all of them."

"Yeah, I thought when they broke his thumb last year the school would get down on 'em. But that didn't happen, did it? Anyway, it's probably not a good idea to talk too long."

"Probably."

"Can you give me a ride?"

Jason hadn't expected this request and didn't know what to say, despite knowing he couldn't do it for more reasons than he could count.

"Where to?"

"I don't know. Somewhere I can catch a bus. Get out of Texas."

"I can't, man. My mom won't let me drive out of town. You know that."

"Just this once?"

The excuses piled up in Jason's mind. It wasn't just his mom. It was the certainty of discovery. She checked the mileage whenever he drove. She'd know right away. And she'd put two and two together and she'd know he'd helped a wanted criminal escape. She'd report it to the police. That's just the way she was. But it sounded so lame. But what else could he say?

"Adan, I really wish I could help but I'm afraid that if I do I'll get caught and they'll put me on trial for helping you. You know, aiding and abetting, like they say on the cop shows."

Adan's silence made things worse.

"Why don't you call Bax? He's got a car. It's a piece of junk but he goes to Beaumont all the time. He's got a job at the grocery store. He's like your biggest fan right now."

"You're sure?"

"Yeah, I'm sure. You got his number?"

"No."

"I'll text you."

13

Adan debated whether to call Baxter. It was late and every moment that passed made the decision more difficult. Few cars had driven by since nightfall, which helped relieve his anxiety about capture. But he was tired, thirsty and hungry. And he was concerned that Baxter wouldn't take his call. He didn't know him *that* well. Encouraged by what Jason had told him, however, but uncertain, he sent a text.

Call me when you can. Adan

He included his name just to be certain that Baxter knew who he'd be calling. Already acutely aware of his status as a fugitive, he almost immediately regretted sending the text. What if Baxter turned him in? They hadn't hung out together the way that he and Whitman hung out. They were buds. But Baxter was Whitman's bud, too, just not as much. The three had known each other since middle school, often ate lunch together and commiserated about being picked on. The difference between them was that Baxter always seemed to be working after school. Over the years he'd worked as a dishwasher and busboy and during the summer worked with his mother's boyfriend's roofing company. Then, after getting his driver's license and buying a car, he got a night job in Beaumont stocking shelves. Adan envied him, envied his driver's license, envied his freedom. He could go anywhere anytime he wanted, unlike Jason who had to do whatever his mother required in order to even drive her car to buy milk. Jason was on a tight leash, unlike Baxter.

Adan's regret at sending the text boiled into frustration as minutes passed without a response. Five minutes. Ten minutes. Twenty minutes. Meanwhile, the woods exploded with sounds. Cicadas he knew about, but everything else was unfamiliar and vaguely unnerving, especially the scratching noises from nearby. Every sound captured his attention until he could either convince himself it wasn't a threat or it went away. His imagination needed only a kick-start to go into overdrive, heightening his agitation. The notion of alligators was all it took for him to dig through his duffel bag in search of his grandfather's gun. Fumbling in the dark, under the closeness of the old wool blanket, he inserted the clip in the darkness but didn't chamber a round and made sure the safety was on. He didn't want a repeat of the mistake he'd made at school.

A half hour after sending the text, with no response, armed and ready to defend himself against whatever nature had to offer, he slowly succumbed to his exhaustion, his mind floating like a leaf on a slow-moving stream. The noises of the woods slowly faded into the background until all that remained was the leaf, suspended in silent darkness.

14

ADAN WOKE SOON AFTER A FLOCK OF COMMON grackles homed in on the telephone lines and trees towering over his encampment. Rubbing his unfocused eyes he listened abstractedly to the noisy birds. Everything that had happened the previous day seemed so far away that for a moment he thought he was in the middle of a dream. Then he felt the gun jabbing him in his back as he stretched his lean body, trying to keep his feet from poking out the end. He could use a cup of coffee, he thought, as he came to a sitting position, wrapping the blanket around his shoulders like a shawl. The air was coolish but humid. The grackles filled the air with their harsh calls. Adan couldn't hear himself think but he felt safe for the moment. Now that early daylight had arrived, he saw the road to be farther away than he'd thought and that his campsite was in the midst of thick, tall underbrush.

He saw the text as soon as he looked at his phone. It had popped up a little after midnight. It was now five a.m. The debate restarted. Should he call Baxter now? Was it too early? If he worked late, would that mean he'd be sleeping through the morning? It was Saturday after all. Sleeping through the night had done nothing to relieve Adan's hunger or thirst. He needed help now. The phone's battery was draining with every passing minute. He couldn't afford to lose power now.

Adan pressed the phone against his ear as it rang, once, twice, three times, four. Then five. He wondered if Baxter had voicemail. He wondered whether he should leave a message.

"Hello, hello," Baxter's voice burst on the line. "Is that you, Adan?"

Adan exhaled.

"It's me. How you doin', Bax? Did I wake you?"

"Yeah, but that's OK. Whit told me you were gonna call. I thought it was gonna be last night. But no prob. You get my text?"

"Yeah, but I was asleep. I'm out here in the middle of nowhere. There's a bunch of noisy birds."

"Is that what it is? I thought it was the connection. You know, man, what you did was—"

"A mistake."

"I was gonna say awesome. Sick, man. It was like a dream come true."

Adan sighed.

"Well, now I got a problem."

"I'll bet. What you gonna do?"

"I need a ride. I need to get to a bus station, but not the one in town. They'll be looking there for sure."

"Where you goin'?"

"Anywhere away from here. First bus available. The farther away, the better."

"Where are you now?"

"Off a county road somewhere north of town. Not sure. I can look for a road sign."

"You got GPS?"

"On my phone? It's a flip phone."

"How am I gonna find you?"

With every detail of the previous day and night embedded in his consciousness, Adan described his route.

"I think I know where you are," Baxter said confidently.

"That's great. I really appreciate this."

"No prob, man. You know how that asshole broke my thumb last year, right? Nothin' happened. Nobody cared. Now they'll care."

Adan shook his head. He wasn't proud of what he'd done. He was ashamed and wished it had never happened.

"When you come, can you bring something to drink and something to eat? Anything. I'm starving. Oh, bring some scissors."

"Sure, man. Just be looking for me."

15

AFTER DISCONNECTING, ADAN LAY ON THE BLANKET and let his shoulders settle into the pine needle mattress. He felt relief for the first time since the shooting. Help was on the way. Food and water were on the way. Smiling as he stared at the tree tops, for a moment he forgot that he was a fugitive, that he had spent a fretful night in the woods and that he was leaving his home perhaps never to return. No longer worried about the immediate future, all he wanted to do was lie back, his hands cushioning his head, and fall asleep. It would be so easy. Baxter could wake him, one part of his brain suggested. It wouldn't be long. Just a catnap. What could go wrong?

Another part of his brain sounded an alarm. Startled out of his reverie, he sat up, suddenly wide awake. There was no time to waste. He needed to formulate a plan. Dredging up everything he could recall from crime shows and articles he'd read online, he imagined what the police would be doing to find him and what he could do to make sure they didn't succeed. The bus out of Texas was the touchstone.

He had already decided to ask Baxter to cut his long brown hair. Maybe he could dye it at some point. He'd need a hat or cap, something to disguise what he figured would be a hasty and uneven hairdo. He needed new clothes. His clothes were little more than a uniform—black pants, white t-shirt, white tennis shoes that he'd blackened with shoe polish. Several pairs of everything. He wore collared shirts to school but he'd left them behind. How much effort would the authorities put into his capture if he managed to get out of Texas? How likely was it they would hunt him down wherever he went when the country was filled with murderers, drug dealers and rapists on the run? It just made sense that the farther away he got from Vidor, the less likely anyone would be looking for him.

By the time Baxter arrived, Adan had his duffel bag zipped. He'd kept a watchful eye on the sparse traffic, rushing to the road to wave as he heard the throaty resonance of his friend's truck.

"Man, man," Baxter said enthusiastically as he swung the big metal driver's door open, barely missing Adan, who warily watched the road.

"Am I glad to see you," Adan said gratefully, bumping fists. "I thought you'd never get here."

"It took longer than I thought," Baxter said, reaching for a plastic bag in the front seat.

Adan smiled broadly, grabbed the bag and retreated to his campsite where he washed down Twinkies with warmish coffee from a foam cup.

"I can't tell you how thankful I am for what you're doing," he said between bites. "What do I owe ya for the food?"

"Nothin', man," Baxter said. "It's more like what do I owe you?"

Adan looked puzzled.

"For what you did," he said, holding out his right thumb, which was bent permanently at the knuckle. "See that? What you did was get back at that asshole for what he did to me."

"You got the scissors?"

"In the truck."

"Good. I need you to cut my hair."

"What?"

"I need to change my appearance. I can't do it. I'll screw it up."

"I've never cut anyone's hair before."

"Doesn't matter. Just make it shorter, a lot shorter," Adan said firmly. "By the way, do you have a cap or something I can use?"

"No, bro. I wish you'd asked. I coulda brought one."

"That's OK. Just cut my hair. I don't care what it looks like. Just make it fast. And don't cut me."

16

For a breathless moment, Adan watched as a car approached, headed north at a high rate of speed. Baxter had finished the haircut, loaded Adan's duffel bag onto the truck bed and sat on the edge of the driver's seat.

"Man, that was close," Adan said as he lifted himself into the passenger seat. "I thought for sure that was a cop."

"You're paranoid, huh?"

"Yeah, definitely. It's weird how it makes you feel."

"How what makes you feel?"

"Being on the run. It's like you see danger everywhere."

"Where to?"

"A bus station, but not the one in town. Do you have a map or something?"

"I got one on my phone."

"Can you pull it up? Maybe you can find something nearby, just not in town."

Adan grew agitated while Baxter searched for bus stations.

"You know, we shouldn't park here like this. A cop comes by and he's sure to stop. Why don't we drive down the road until we can find a place to stop, you know, off the road?"

"Looks like the closest station is in Port Arthur."

"Wrong way, man," Adan said. "I need to be going north or east, out of Texas."

"OK, OK, what do you want to do first? Move or find a bus station?"

"Maybe I can look it up on your phone while you drive. How's that?"

"OK, that'll work. I'll just drive until we find a place to stop. There's bound to be a gas station or convenience store."

It didn't take long for Adan to realize that finding a bus station was more complicated than he had thought. The nearest Greyhound station was in Lake Charles, Louisiana, less than an hour's drive on Interstate 10. They'd been driving for about five minutes when Adan told Baxter to turn around.

"Where to?"

"Lake Charles," Adan said.

"Cool."

Finally, the problem was solved and Adan enjoyed a moment of relief. By six thirty, the two young men were on Interstate 10 headed toward Louisiana, the sun low, intense and in their eyes. Traffic was light as they drove the speed limit with the windows down, warm, moist air rushing through the cab, the driver smiling, the passenger muted, his head propped against the door frame and the seat back. Adan's mind was racing, trying to anticipate everything that could go wrong. He wanted to ask whether Baxter's truck had a faulty taillight but didn't. He eyed the speedometer but the driver had that under control, staying in the right lane, even slowing for vehicles trying to enter traffic.

Nothing to draw attention, he hoped, his eyes surveying the road behind and in front of them for police cars. Surely, he wondered, they wouldn't set up a road block? But the tension he'd felt before they had settled on a destination melted and with it some of his hypervigilance and the adrenaline that supported it. For a moment, he felt relaxed. Normal. As if there was nothing to worry about.

17

Adan had never purchased a bus ticket on his own. The few times he and his grandfather had traveled by bus, the old man bought the tickets. But he felt apprehensive as they pulled into the sprawling truck stop at Lake Charles, as if he'd forgotten something. No, that wasn't it. He hadn't forgotten anything. Still, he felt uncertain about what would come next. Something he hadn't thought of. Adan exhaled loudly as Baxter parked the truck.

"What's up?" Baxter asked.

"I don't know," Adan said, quietly. "I just feel kinda jittery."

"Maybe it's all that sugar you ate. The Twinkies."

"I don't think that's it."

"You afraid?"

"I don't know. All of a sudden it's like I don't know what I'm gonna do, you know?"

"I can only imagine. I mean, your whole life has changed, right? You're not thinking of going back to town, are you?"

"I thought about it. But I'm seventeen. They'd try me as an adult. Besides, I can't afford a lawyer."

"You know what they say. *If you can't afford a lawyer one will be appointed for you,*" Baxter said, trying to imitate a character from *Law and Order.*

"I've seen all the shows. Court appointed attorneys get paid crap. It's not like they're looking for poor people to represent. I'll end up in prison just like my dad. I just know it."

Baxter eyed Adan with sympathy and admiration. Adan had done something that Baxter had fantasized about but could never do. There was always a voice in the back of his head that cautioned against acting out. Thinking about it was OK, but nothing more. Sitting in the presence of one who did act out, he felt uncomfortable with the realization that Adan would like nothing more than that it had never happened. Of course, he wasn't thinking of his role in aiding and abetting Adan's escape. Were he pulled over by law enforcement he'd be on the hook for the crime as much as Adan. But he was thinking of Adan, feeling sorry for him.

"Still got the gun?" Baxter asked, to change the subject.

"Yeah, I don't know what to do with it. Should I throw it away? I don't know."

"That's what they do on the crime shows. The ones who get caught always have their gun. 'Course, they catch the ones who tossed their guns, too. So, I don't know. You think you'll need it?"

"I hope not. I don't want it if I don't need it."

"But if you need it, you want it?"

"Yeah. But if I get caught with a gun, that'll just make things worse," Adan said, irritated. "There's just no good answer, I guess. Anyway, how about I buy you breakfast?"

"How much time you got?"

"According to the schedule," he said, holding up his phone, "the next bus for St. Louis leaves at 7:55 a.m. Tomorrow."

18

"So, what're you gonna do?"

"I'm still looking," Adan said anxiously, scrolling through Baxter's phone while waiting for breakfast.

They'd moved Adan's duffel bag from the truck bed into the cab, locking it behind them. The only bus he could find out of Lake Charles that wasn't headed back to Texas was a 3:55 to New Orleans, two hundred miles to the east. It meant spending nearly half the day at the truck stop, waiting. But that was better than spending the night waiting for the bus to St. Louis. Adan wasn't good at waiting. He got antsy. But scrolling through the Greyhound web site brought up other complications, such as identification, which was required. The boarding pass included the purchaser's name.

"Fuck," Adan said under his breath as both sipped coffee.

"What now?"

"I can't get a ticket without ID."

"Definitely not good."

"I wonder if the cops are checking Lake Charles? I can

see why they'd check Vidor's bus station, but this is kinda far away. Don't you think?"

"I don't know, man. With computers they can do anything."

They stopped talking for several minutes after the food arrived. Both ordered pancakes with sides of bacon.

"You know, I hate to ask, but can you buy the ticket for me?"

"You gonna go to New Orleans?" Baxter asked, concentrating on his pancakes.

"We're about the same size and they prolly won't check closely anyway," Adan said, handing the phone to Baxter.

"What're you gonna do when you get there?"

"You don't wanna do it? I mean, I wouldn't blame you. You've done a lot already."

Baxter looked up from his plate and blew a puff of air toward Adan.

"I don't know, man."

"They can't connect you to me," Adan said, making his case. "They ain't looking for your name. You can buy a ticket and just say you changed your mind and threw it away, or gave it to a homeless person. Nobody'll even know."

"What if you get caught? My name'll be on the ticket, right?"

"You can tell 'em I stole your driver's license. I won't get you into trouble."

Baxter looked at his phone, as if expecting to find an answer to Adan's question.

"I wonder what homeless people do? They don't have ID. Do they?" Baxter asked.

Adan shrugged. The person who had enabled his escape now seemed to be standing in the way of it. One more favor was all that he needed. He could hang out in the truck stop until the bus arrived.

"What if you need to show ID when you board?"

"I couldn't find anything on the web site. But why would they do that? Seems like that would just slow things down. The last time I rode a bus the driver was the only person to help people get on, and he was busy loading and unloading cargo and all that. And just look at this place; it ain't what you expect a bus station to look like."

Baxter rapped his fingers on the table top, his eyebrows knitted, his lips tightly drawn. Adan watched expectantly, wondering what he would do if Baxter wouldn't buy the ticket.

"OK, OK," Baxter whispered, "I'll buy the fucking ticket."

"Great. Let's finish here. I'll pay. Wait for me in the truck."

As Baxter left, Adan went to a rack of billed hats and grabbed one embellished with the New Orleans Saints fleur-de-lis logo on the front, paying for it along with the cost of the meal. Returning to the table he dropped a pair of ones and joined Baxter out front.

"So, you're a Saints fan now?"

Adan nodded, pulled out his wallet and handed a pair of twenties to Baxter.

"OK, go buy the ticket. I'll wait here. But could you unlock the truck first?"

While Baxter was gone, Adan reached inside of the cab, rummaged through his duffel bag, and pulled out the wad of his grandfather's cash. He took out five twenties, folded them and tucked them into a front pocket of his blue jeans. It was hot, humid and breezy, the sun encouraging him to put on his shades. Briefly, he watched himself in a reflection on a truck stop window. Shadows from the hat's bill combined with the sunglasses to hide much of his face. If he kept his head down, someone who knew him might walk right by and not recognize him. Originally, he'd thought he needed to get far away from Texas but now that he thought about it, New Orleans would be fine. It was hundreds of miles from home. Nobody knew him there. And everything he had ever heard about the city made him think it would be easy to get by.

"Hey, man," Baxter said as he returned, boarding pass in hand.

"Any trouble?"

"Are you kidding? I don't think the guy even looked at my driver's license. I held it up but he just asked me my name and keyboarded it. Hell, I coulda given any name."

"That's great, Bax. I can't tell ya how much I appreciate what you've done for me. I mean, if it weren't for you, I'd probably be in jail right now. Or dead."

Adan reached into his pants pocket and palmed the currency.

"I want you to have this," he said, holding the money between his thumb and forefinger.

"Man, I can't take that," Baxter protested. "You're gonna need it. I got a job and I'm not on the lam like you. Just keep it."

"At least let me pay for gas and the stuff you bought."

"Adan," Baxter said, putting his hand on the young fugitive's shoulder, "I appreciate what you did, and I'm sure I'm not the only one. Keep your money. Keep out of trouble."

The two fist-bumped and then hugged. Adan stood in front of the truck with his duffel bag and watched until his friend disappeared down the frontage road, headed west.

19

THE HOURS CRAWLED AS ADAN ANXIOUSLY WAITED FOR the 3:55 to New Orleans. At first, he feared that he would draw attention, a young guy with a duffel bag moving in and out of the truck stop, buying a soft drink here, a snack there, until he realized that the workers were more interested in talking to each other than watching strangers. Employees were accustomed to seeing people loitering, waiting for a bus. Some of them came with suitcases, others with cardboard boxes. Some had nothing but the clothes they wore.

Adan searched for a place outdoors where he could sack out on his duffel bag and catch up on lost sleep. But the only shade was under the huge awnings covering the fuel pumps. The now blazing sun kept him away from the narrow concrete walkway in front of the building and though he enjoyed the relief that came with being inside, he felt uneasy taking up a seat in the restaurant without buying something. By eleven o'clock he'd had enough to eat and drink to last him the day and still it seemed forever before the bus would arrive. He bought a local newspaper from a rack near the automobile fuel pumps, apprehensively paging through it, expecting to find a story and photo detailing the shooting. Buried on an inside page was a two paragraph item in which the victim and the perpetrator were described as students. No names. No photos. Running away seemed to be a successful strategy, he thought, smiling as he leaned against a back wall of the building, squeezing himself into a narrow band of shade. He read the article several times, as if he'd overlooked a key word or sentence. He hadn't. It was a nothing story.

The population of loiterers increased as the departure time neared. Adan counted ten people on his most recent circuit of the building, most of them black. He'd spent so little time among blacks that he found himself sitting on the concrete in front of the building studying them, listening to them, catching a phrase here, a word there. He could never tell when his grandfather talked about blacks whether he was afraid of them or repelled by them. Vidor was as white as any town in the country and for most of his life he never gave it a thought. Now, though, he was no longer in Vidor. And most of what he'd read online or been told about Katrina and New Orleans tended to reinforce his grandfather's racism. At the moment, however, it was not a good time to be thinking about what Harley had told him. He had to start thinking about his future and right now that would be occurring in New Orleans, a city where blacks outnumbered whites two to one.

Even before he boarded the bus, his mind worked to come up with a survival strategy. Although only seventeen, he'd had to take care of himself from the day his grandfather became his guardian. Over the years he'd learned how to avoid being victimized by Harley's rages, which sometimes took a physical turn but mostly involved shouting and threats. He'd gotten accustomed to seeing him burst into tirades watching network news, especially coverage of Black Lives Matter or civil rights, or talking about the old days when Vidor was a proper Sundown Town. It was a wonder to him that the old man hadn't taken a shotgun to the TV, but as quick to anger as he was, he had enough self-control to avoid harming himself or his property.

As much as he didn't like it, Adan debated whether to change his identity. Not just cutting his hair and wearing a hat but the kind of sophisticated tactics that he'd seen on TV. He couldn't use his own Social Security number for two reasons. One, he wasn't certain that he remembered it correctly and, two, the authorities might be able to track him down if it popped up somewhere. He knew from TV that criminals used Social Security numbers of people who died at a young age. They didn't just make them up. But he was at a loss of how to do it. He couldn't imagine doing it himself but he figured that having a new identity in a city where no one had heard of him would allow him to disappear in plain sight.

Once he started thinking like this, he couldn't stop. One thought led to another, and another, until the process seemed so daunting and endless that he would never get through it. Should he discard his phone? It was his only connection with his friends but also a connection the police could use to track him. Where would he sleep when he got to New Orleans? Should he get rid of his student ID? Keeping it was too risky, he thought. It tied him directly to his past. And what about the gun?

But relief came when he saw the big bus turn into the truck stop. All his worries vanished like forgotten dreams. He quickly got in line with other passengers who were waiting to board. The driver barely looked at him as he collected his boarding pass. Settling into the assigned window seat, he felt as if he'd finally arrived at a safe place, though, as he stared out the tinted window at the dwindling queue of riders, he felt an instant of panic as his mind dredged up another familiar scene from cop shows—a criminal being arrested after boarding a bus. A quick peek at the parking lot eased his mind and when the bus started moving he glanced at the older black man who sat alongside him and smiled.

The man smelled of lavender.

20

THE ONLY THING THAT CAME EASILY TO ADAN AFTER arriving in New Orleans was stepping off the bus. From that moment forward he found himself bouncing from one homeless enclave to another, struggling to survive without breaking the law, struggling to blend in, struggling with his own doubts and contradictions.

It didn't take him long to learn not to trust anyone. From the start, he knew he would need an ID of some sort and a Social Security number. He also knew that he could not use his real name to obtain these things. During nights sleeping with other homeless he learned of a man who could provide what he needed for a price.

"He's a big black guy who wears one of those knit hats," he was told. "You might find him selling stuff to tourists at Armstrong Park. His name's Cornel."

While walking around with a duffel bag wasn't unusual among the homeless, Adan realized that it was viewed suspiciously by others. He could see it in their eyes when they passed by. They'd give him an unmistakable second look. It didn't help that he hadn't bathed and his clothing was wrinkled. He couldn't very well leave the bag where he'd slept. And without ID, he couldn't get into any of the homeless shelters he'd tried, even for a night. Ironically, in the evening when restaurants gave their leftovers to the homeless, the duffel bag was his ID. Nobody handing out food or water questioned whether a man with a duffel bag was homeless.

It took several days but he finally found a big black man wearing a white kufi sitting on a bench in the park, with an array of trinkets and voodoo items spread out on a blanket in front of him. He sold voodoo dolls he made out of Spanish moss, sticks and bits of cloth, added food coloring to cooking oil that he sold in tiny bottles as money oil, and gris-gris bags, all of which he sold much cheaper than local shops. Cornel didn't even look up as Adan walked by, sizing up the man in the kufi. On Adan's second pass, Cornel spoke up.

"Say, there, unless you're buying something move on. You'll scare away my customers."

Adan stopped in front of the bench, pulling on the thin soul patch that, along with an uneven mustache, made him look older than seventeen.

"Any of that stuff work?" Adan asked, pausing in front of Cornel's display.

"You gotta buy it to try it," he grinned.

"I'm told you can help me with an ID, get an ID card."

"Who told you this?"

"I don't know his name. I'm new in town."

Cornel grinned broadly, his teeth bright white in the sun. Adan thought he had a friendly smile.

"What's your name?"

"Adan."

"You got a last name?"

"Burke. What's your name?"

"Cornel Whitehead. Now tell me, Adan Burke, why would a young white man need an ID? Don't you have a birth certificate?"

Adan snickered.

"I get it. You think a black man named Whitehead is funny. Is that it?"

"Yeah, sorta funny. To answer your question, I can't get it."

"And why is that?"

Adan hadn't told anyone in New Orleans he was running from the law, not that anyone he'd met would care. They were all struggling with life in their own way. He believed half the homeless people he met were mentally ill or doing a good job faking it. Adan thought about walking away but he knew he needed an ID more than anything else.

"I was told you could get me an ID and a Social Security number."

"Maybe I can and maybe I can't," Whitehead said stiffly. "How old are you?"

"Nineteen," Adan lied.

"Hmmf. Where you from?

"Texas."

"I can tell from your accent you're from Texas," Whitehead said, irritated. "What city?"

"Dallas," Adan lied again.

"You're pretty young to need an ID. Did you kill someone?"

"Nothing like that. Look, maybe I'll just go. Sorry to bother you."

Glancing around to check for eavesdroppers, Whitehead motioned for Adan to stay.

"Don't be that way. I'm just trying to know who I'm dealing with."

"How do I know you won't turn me in? How do I know you're not a cop?"

"Do I look like a snitch to you?" he said, offended.

"How do I know you ain't lying?"

"You're really a smart ass, aren't you? For a guy who wants my help, you're not making it easy. Let me tell you something, everyone lies. Everyone. Everywhere. Ain't just a Nawlins thing. You probably lying right now. Am I right?"

Adan adjusted his duffel bag, which was slung over his shoulder, and started slowly to move away.

"OK," Whitehead said. "I know a guy who can do this for you but it'll cost you two hundred fifty dollars. The fifty's for me and the two hundred for him. Payable in advance."

Adan set his duffel bag on the ground and furtively ruffled through it, turning his back to Whitehead so that he wouldn't see the wad of cash. Aside from money he'd spent on food before learning that he could get free handouts, the cash hoard was intact. He held out three fifties and five twenties, startling Whitehead.

"Put that away," he said gruffly, looking around to see if anyone was watching. "You don't just hand out cash like that. Cops could be watching. Fuck, you hand a bunch of notes to a black man and they think I'm selling drugs."

"But you're not selling drugs. Besides, I don't see anybody."

"Don't matter if they see you. Gives them probable cause. Don't you know anything?"

Adan stuffed the bills into his pocket and watched as Whitehead rose and walked toward a stand of shade trees fifty feet behind the bench. Adan slowly followed.

"All right. Now just hand me the money and I'll get you your ID."

"And a Social Security number," Adan said quickly.

"Of course. That's what we discussed."

Adan hesitated before handing the money over.

"When will I get the ID?"

"Usually takes a coupla days. Week at the most. You wanna use your own name or something else?"

Adan hadn't given any thought to what name to use. If he got stopped and the police did a name search, his name would pop up as a fugitive, he was certain of it.

"I think I should use a different name."

"So, you done something wrong back in Texas and you're on the run," Whitehead said.

Adan nodded.

"Well, it don't matter. No way to trace it to me, unless you talk and I can always make it he said-he said. Got a name in mind, Adan Burke?"

Adan rubbed his chin, a concerned look on his face.

"No big deal," Whitehead prodded. "Any old name will do when it's fake. I can make something up if you want. Don't want to stand around here all day."

Adan's mind bogged down. All he could think of were names of people he knew.

"You can pick a name," Adan said. "Just don't make it weird or hard to spell. Where do I find you?"

"I'm here and there. Got my business to run, as you see," Whitehead said, nodding toward his blanket of trinkets.

"Yeah, but where will I find you?"

"Got a phone?"

"Nope. Threw it away."

"Well, you need to get yourself a phone, stay in touch

with people," Whitehead said. "OK. Let's assume it's ready by Friday. You can find me here around noon. Same place."

Adan wanted to ask if Whitehead was going to rip him off but thought better of it as he gave the currency to him, who quickly buried the folded bills in his pants pocket. Pulling out a cell phone from his shirt pocket, he clicked on a camera app and aimed it at Adan, who stepped back in surprise.

"Need your pitcher for the ID," Whitehead said as he snapped several photos.

"Aren't you gonna count it?" Adan asked as Cornel finished.

"Why? If you try to stiff me, I'll stiff you."

As Adan started to leave, Whitehead said, "One more thing. Take a shower, man. You're ripe."

21

THE BENCH WAS EMPTY WHEN ADAN RETURNED TO THE park early Friday afternoon. Taking a position near where he'd given Cornel the cash, he watched the bench from the shade. One o'clock. Two o'clock. Three o'clock. Four o'clock. No Cornel. Adan returned to the park twice only to find that Whitehead wasn't there. Finally, he concluded that the person who had told him about Cornel was working with him and the pair had ripped him off. It frustrated him to no end as he sat in the shade watching and waiting for White-head until finally giving up, blaming himself for being stupid and naive and vowing never to trust anyone again.

More than anything after three weeks in New Orleans Adan missed having someone he could trust to talk to. Lying awake at night amidst other homeless, wrapped in his scratchy blanket, he thought about getting in touch with his best friend, Jason Whitman. It helped to let his mind drift away from the circumstances surrounding him, the noise, the petty arguments he couldn't avoid overhearing, the smell of urine and rotting garbage. The fear that someone would try to rob him or hurt him in his sleep. Fear of robbery was always on his mind, which is why during the daytime he kept to more or less public places. Other homeless warned him to stay away from certain neighborhoods, Little Woods, Central City and others. They also said the French Quarter was known for assaults, but that's where he'd spent most of his time in the beginning and didn't feel unsafe. He believed most crime happened at night.

After being ripped off by Whitehead, Adan learned that he couldn't even get a library card without some form of ID. He'd tossed his school ID along with his phone when he arrived, eliminating the only direct connection to his former life in Vidor. He'd never been fingerprinted nor DNA'd. In an effort to stow his duffel bag, he located a storage company where he could rent a small unit cheaply. When the subject of identification came up, he took a form to fill out and never came back.

The more he tried, the more he realized that without ID, he wouldn't be able to get a job or gain admittance to a homeless shelter. Even though he still had more than half his cash, desperation was building like a slowly developing thunderstorm. He needed to talk to someone he could trust.

22

Jason Whitman didn't recognize the number when his phone vibrated on his desk, the ring tone off so as not to disturb his mother, who had fallen asleep in the living room. His mind was on the video he was watching on his computer so he didn't answer it. Fifteen minutes later he heard a ping. A voicemail had come through. His curiosity piqued, he paused the video and listened to the brief message. It was from Adan Burke.

"What the fuck?" Whitman whispered to himself. It had been three weeks since he'd seen Adan. Billy Baxter had told him about driving Adan to Lake Charles to catch a bus. His instinct was to return the call immediately, but he hesitated, stepping into the hallway and peeking into the living room to make sure his mom was still asleep. Quietly, he shut his bedroom door behind him and listened to the voicemail a second time.

"Call me," was the extent of it.

It was nearly ten o'clock on a school night but there was no choice to be made between finishing the video and returning the call.

Adan knew Jason's number and could barely contain himself when he answered his phone. The conversation started out one sided, with Jason blurting out question after question, leaving no opportunity for responses.

"It's really good to hear your voice," Adan said, finally. "Are they still looking for me, the police?"

"You won't believe what's been going on. Bax told me all about your trip. You're in New Orleans now, right?"

Adan hesitated.

"You're not bugged, right?"

"Bugged? The cops didn't even talk to me. Besides, turns out that after what you did all kinds of kids came out of the woodwork to complain about the bullying. You would not believe it. In fact, we had an assembly about it."

"No kidding. But, what about me? Are they still looking for me?"

"Oh, I don't know. That's old news now. There was a big wreck on the interstate the day you left and then a bunch of other stuff happened."

"Did they identify me in the newspaper?"

"I'm not sure. We don't get the paper."

"How about TV?"

"Not sure. You can check it out on the internet. I searched on your name and it only popped up a couple times."

"I just got this phone. Things have been tough."

"You're OK, right? Are you coming back?"

"I'd like to, but I can't. I don't want to go to jail. I had a nightmare where my dad and me were in the same cell and Gramps was beating us with his belt."

The two fell silent for a moment, Whitman not certain what to say and Adan trying to block out noise from nearby traffic.

"Where are you?" Whitman asked. "Sounds noisy."

"I'm near an overpass. Had to get in the open to get a signal."

Adan summarized the bad things that had happened to him since arriving in New Orleans, especially his attempt to get an ID.

"It's harder than I thought. You gotta have ID to get ID, or you gotta know someone who won't rip you off. I will say, if I ever see that guy again, I'm gonna get my money back. He really fucked things up for me. I thought I'd have a shit job by now. The only thing good is some of the restaurants here give out leftovers after they close. Good food, too."

"Do any dumpster diving?"

"Nope. Haven't had to, but I suppose I would if I was hungry enough. I'll tell you, living on the street ain't easy."

"Not in the Big Easy, huh?"

"Not at all," Adan said, pausing. "Anyway, I was wondering if you maybe could call my gramps and see if he would get a copy of my birth certificate."

Jason froze momentarily, as if he'd been asked to jump off a cliff.

"Man, I'm afraid of your grampa. He's mean."

"Yeah, but just a phone call?"

"Why don't you call him? You've got a phone."

"I'm afraid, too. I took half his money and I still got his gun."

"Wait a minute. If you use your birth certificate, wouldn't that make it easier for the cops to find you?"

Adan groaned.

"Yeah, but I'm running out of money and I need to get a job."

"I'll think about it," Jason said disingenuously. "No promises. He scares the shit out of me."

Adan saw that Jason wouldn't help but didn't want the conversation to end on a low note.

"That's fine. Think about it. I better get goin'. Look, it was great talking to you."

"Me, too. Good luck," Jason said before realizing that Adan had already disconnected.

23

At first, Adan sought safety in numbers. He was the new guy and he thought he'd watch the veteran homeless and possibly learn something about surviving on the streets. Some were helpful, pointing out where to get food handouts and the location of public restrooms. Others just didn't seem right in the head. The hard thing was telling them apart. During the day, they wandered on their own, trying to stay out of trouble or at least avoid encounters with police, only to return to their nightly roost where even the most trivial conversation could turn into an argument without warning. Sometimes knives were drawn. It was times like that that Adan was glad he still had his grandfather's gun. Even though it was buried in his duffel bag and would be hard to find on a moment's notice, knowing it was there made him feel safer.

The week after his encounter with Whitehead, and after watching and listening to the bickering, the shouting matches, the threats, the junkies laid out like mannequins and after coming close to being assaulted himself, he moved on, having found not one person who seemed interested in becoming his friend, though he did have a conversation about other places to sleep with a guy who claimed to be a government agent. The only person Adan knew by name was Cornel Whitehead, who he'd been told was peddling his wares somewhere near St. Louis Cathedral.

"When I get so I want to be alone, I sleep in da doorway in da Quarter. You jes' wait till they close and set yourself up in the doorway."

"In front?"

"Of course, in front. Where you think the door is? Boy, you OK?"

"Well, I just thought maybe it's better to sleep in the back, you know, where there's more privacy."

"Privacy? There's plenty streets where nobody goes at night. Ain't all bad ones neither. Stay away from the life, you know. No houses. They might shoot you. But nobody cares if you sleep in a doorway of a business. Jes' don't make trouble. I hardly been rousted once. You got a dolla?"

The man held his hand out.

"Hey, I'm homeless just like you," Adan said, surprised.

"You ain't jes' like me. I'm a government agent and I'm s'posed to collect da fee to cover my expenses. It's in the agent's manual. Says I should panhandle to blend in. Now, you got a dolla?"

Adan dropped four quarters into the man's hand.

"Hey, what you trying to put over on me?" he asked testily. "I aksed for a dollar."

"OK, OK," Adan said as he held out his hand to retrieve the coins.

"Hey, diss is mine," the agent said defensively. "You still owe me a dolla. You don't give it to me and you can forget everything I tole you. You cain't use it, you unnerstand. You hafta give it back 'cause otherwise it's stealin'."

Adan walked away quickly after giving the man a crumpled Washington. It was mid-afternoon and, lugging his duffel bag across his shoulder, he walked up and down several streets, making mental notes of the store fronts. Then his phone rang. He didn't recognize the number but it had Vidor's 409 area code.

"How'd anyone get my number?" he mumbled as he turned a corner and set his bag on the ground next to the shady side of a two-story brick building. He sat on his bag, his back against the wall, for several minutes, waiting for his phone to ring. When it came, he waited several more minutes until the voicemail icon lit up. If it wasn't Jason Whitman, who could it be? *The cops* was the first thing that popped into his head. Maybe they questioned Whitman. Maybe there was a reward and Whitman wanted to collect it. Suddenly, he saw nothing but the worst in his best friend but quickly scolded himself for doing so. He was the only best friend he'd ever had. Jason wouldn't do that. It had to be someone else.

He was fearful of playing the message, as if by doing so he would be endangering himself.

But he couldn't resist.

"Hi, Adan," the boyish voice said, "this is your partner in crime, Bax. Gimme a call when you can. I talked to your grampa."

24

"WHIT CALLED ME," BILLY BAXTER SAID AFTER answering Adan's call. "He's such a pussy. He told me what you told him and I told him I'd call your grampa."

"You did?"

"Oh, yeah. I can see why everybody's afraid of him. I thought he was gonna punch me in the mouth through the phone when I mentioned your name."

"I was afraid of that."

"You doin' all right?"

"I'm gettin' by, but it's really hard if you don't have ID. I can't get into a shelter or anything. Been sleeping on the street. Well, not literally, but under bridges and places where other people sleep. A lot of crazy shit goin' on here. Did Jason tell you I got ripped off?"

"No."

"I guess I didn't tell him. Yeah, I paid a guy two hundred and fifty bucks to get me an ID card but I haven't been able to track him down. I guess Gramps isn't gonna help me, huh?"

"No way. He's pissed. He says you stole all his money and because of you the cops confiscated all his guns."

"I didn't take all his money," Adan said, emphatically.

"I'm just repeating what he said."

"I took half of it. And I left a note."

"He didn't say anything about a note but he said the cops came into the house and did a search."

"Maybe the cops took it. It wasn't me. Shit."

"I tried to help, man."

"I know. I appreciate that. You helped me a lot."

"Maybe you should call him. Tell him you didn't take all the money and that you left a note."

Adan wanted to ask Baxter to call Harley but couldn't. It was something he would have to do himself. He couldn't spend the rest of his life knowing his grandfather didn't know where the money went.

"So, he actually answered the phone?"

"Yeah, not right away. I guess he screens his calls."

"Yeah, all he gets are sales calls."

"Did Whit tell ya about what happened at school, with the bullying?"

"He said they held an assembly."

"Yep, and so many kids came out to complain about Dearborn and his pals that the principal put all of them in the alternative school for the rest of the semester."

"Wow!"

"Yeah, it's amazing. And just think, if you hadn't done what you did, they'd still be bullying kids."

25

ADAN TRIED TO MAKE FRIENDS BUT NO ONE WAS interested. He had nothing to offer. Conversations seemed to go haywire quickly in a miasma of misunderstanding, mispronunciations, deep south accents and the New Orleans Yat that seemed to result in a vocabulary all their own. More often than not he'd get into a conversation with another homeless person only to listen to him go off on a tangent that wouldn't stop until he walked away.

The loneliness weighed on him more than his duffel bag. He'd always been something of a loner, mostly because of things he couldn't change, such as his grandfather and felon father. Mostly it was guilt by association. But guilt nonetheless. Made him feel inferior. The second-hand clothing, the shoes that never quite fit, the amateurish hair-cuts his grandfather gave him. It all took its toll over the years. Although he hadn't planned it to work out this way, now that he had no choice but to flee to New Orleans he longed for a fresh start not burdened by his past. But it wasn't easy. He couldn't even start until he had some form of identification.

Jason Whitman knew what Adan was talking about. He was an outsider at school, too. The group included him, Adan, Baxter and other kids who for whatever reason were excluded from the herd by the herd. But it was hardest on Adan because he lived on the outskirts of town in a derelict house on a derelict street and had to walk everywhere he went, which was OK until his peers turned sixteen and started driving cars, making a big show of it, while he wore out his soles.

"I don't know what it is about me, but it's hard for me to make friends," he'd confessed to Jason. "It makes me think there's something wrong with me. It makes me think I'm not good enough. My gramps always told me I wouldn't amount to anything. I don't think he was being mean when he said it. He was just being honest."

Jason was a good listener whose only solution was to encourage his friend to graduate from high school and then get the hell out of town, though now that he'd gotten out of town Adan wondered whether it was good advice. But he knew he had no choice. In some ways, his life had taken on a life of its own.

26

WANDERING IN NEW ORLEANS HELPED TO GIVE ADAN the lay of the land. He was beginning to know things about the city. He did some of the things tourists did. He rode the street cars. He went up and down every street in the French Quarter, many times, until without thinking about it he knew where things were. Not like a native but better than a tourist. He watched the Steamboat Natchez ply the Mississippi on its brief voyages, wanting to ride her himself but unable to find a safe place to store his bag. He could stuff the remainder of his cash into his pockets. And if someone stole the bag, all they would get was a bunch of second-hand clothing and the bag itself, all of which he could replace. However, it was the gun that kept him from leaving it unattended. The gun was both his one indisputable strength and his greatest weakness. Even though it was the one material thing that connected him to his crime, having it made him feel safer at night when things sometimes got dicey. Lots of homeless people had knives. But he hadn't seen any guns, though he had heard gunshots at night. This was a debate that wouldn't go away. If only he had someone to talk to about it, someone who could point him in the right direction. But who could possibly do that?

He broke down his problem into smaller parts. The bag was one thing. The gun another. He thought about throwing it into the river but couldn't countenance the finality of it. What if he needed it?

What if he hid the gun and took his chances with the duffel? The gun was small. He could put it in a plastic bag, dig a hole somewhere when no one was looking, cover it up and go on his way, no longer connected to the weapon but knowing where he could find it if he needed it. This was the solution he came up with after watching tourists happily board the paddleboat. What better place to hide the gun than somewhere along the river?

What a relief it was. With that problem solved, it was only natural that the subject of his other big problem came up—his need for identification. He'd been looking off and on for Whitehead once it became apparent that the man had either moved on or ripped him off. He wanted to give him the benefit of the doubt, if only because it meant he hadn't thrown away his money, and he'd been asking around where he could find him when he was told by someone who claimed to know Cornel that he'd seen him around Jackson Square.

"Why you aks?"

"He owes me money."

"He sells trinkets and shit. Why does he owe you money?"

"It was for something else."

The man eyed Adan suspiciously.

"Well, I've known Cornel a long time and if you're worried about your money just know he don't steal. He's a whatchamacallit, an entrepreneur. Don't need to steal. Got his fingers in a lotta little pies."

Still feeling energized from solving the gun problem, Adan headed toward Jackson Square for a change of scenery and the possibility that Whitehead would be there. He wasn't sure whether to believe anything he'd been told, since he'd learned almost from his first night in town that homeless people lie all the time, just like everyone else. He felt so good that he treated himself to a Lucky Dog from a vendor on Decatur Street before climbing the stairs of the Moonwalk overlooking Jackson Square and St. Louis Cathedral. Leaning on the railing and squinting as he scanned the plaza he wondered what the odds were that he would solve his two biggest problems on the same day.

"Cornel, where are you?" he whispered to himself.

27

Using a tourist map, Adan pounded the pavement, having resolved to return to the riverfront to hide his gun that evening. He could not escape the knowledge of his guilt. The longer he'd been in the city, the greater his fear of detection. It would take only one incident and then his freedom would be over. Knowing how his dad ended up in prison, how unfair it was and how all he was doing was defending himself against an attacker led him to believe that any encounter with police would end badly. Fortunately, these things were not on his mind as he wandered through one tourist area after another, starting with the area around Jackson Square.

Every inch of his modest frame exposed his scruffiness. His seventeen-year-old facial hair erupted like sparse weeds across his face. He looked as if he'd slept in his clothing because he had, for days. And he had an aroma about him that caused some people to sniff the air as he passed. But he was on a mission that took him up and down Canal Street several times and finally a long hike to Frenchmen Street, which turned out to be a total bust. Returning to the

Jackson Square neighborhood, and repurposing his mission toward locating a place to spend the night, he walked slowly, eyeing the doorways of every commercial building as if one of them would have his name on it. Turning the corner on Royal Street behind the Place de Henriette Delille, he slowly made his way past several artists whose wares hung from the park's iron fence. Near a sign announcing that the street was closed until 4 p.m., sitting at a small table amid the comings and goings of scores of tourists, was the man Adan knew as Cornel Whitehead.

"Remember me?" Adan said sternly as he set his duffel bag heavily on the sidewalk.

Whitehead looked up, smiling.

"Of course I remember you. You're the young man who needs an ID card. I suppose you think I've ripped you off. Well, let me tell you I haven't."

"I went back to the park and you weren't there," Adan retorted.

"Ah, yes, Louis Armstrong. Business dried up there so I went elsewhere. Been doing fairly well here this week. But you never know. Things change. Got to adapt."

After weeks believing that he'd been ripped off, for some reason, now that he'd located his quarry, he wasn't angry. Perhaps it was the way Whitehead talked that deflected Adan's instinct to get even. Soft-spoken baritone, friendly, the cap resting stylishly on his large head, nothing about him suggested to Adan defensiveness or that he had swindled him.

"Help me close up shop," Whitehead said. "It's goin' on four o'clock. Need to get outta here."

Adan did as he was asked, holding open a salesman's case into which Whitehead carefully stored his effigies and other homemade voodoo paraphernalia.

"This is the most uncomfortable stool I've ever used," he said, folding it into its nylon bag.

"Why do you use it?"

"It's lightweight. Some of the others are a pain to carry around. But my butt's too big," Whitehead said, smiling. "Don't say nothing. I'm tired. Been in the sun too long."

"Now that you're packed up, you got my money?" Adan said hurriedly, as if he couldn't wait to get it out.

"No, I don't have your money."

Adan bristled while Whitehead reached into his back pocket, pulling out a wallet.

"I got an ID card and a Social Security for you," Whitehead said proudly. "You said you wanted a driver's license but I figured you're living on the street so I got an official looking Louisiana ID card. Coulda got a driver's license, but any cop looks at you and he's gonna wonder. Not many homeless people have driver's licenses."

Adan greedily accepted the cards and studied them. He knew what Social Security cards looked like and how the paper felt and the card that Cornel handed him looked genuine. The ID card looked authentic but he'd never seen one.

"This ID card, it looks like a real one?"

"It is a real one, except it ain't. You might notice that I added a coupla years. You're now twenty-one, Justin Baker."

"Why Justin Baker?"

"You look like a Justin. The last name? I was walking past a bakery before I met my man."

28

ADAN HAD THE NOTION THAT GETTING AN ID HAD solved all his problems. It hadn't. The shelters he knew about were already filled for the night and his dilemma was to find a doorway to spend the night. After wrapping the gun in several plastic bags he picked out of a trash can, Adan returned to the riverfront to hide his weapon but it seemed a pedestrian or a cyclist was always passing by, making him apprehensive and too skittish to even take the gun out of his duffel. Having spent much of the day walking in search of Whitehead, he was tired, and as evening turned into night he sat on a bench overlooking the river while finishing a bag of potato chips, washing it down with a bottle of water that he refilled every chance he got.

After an hour of wandering he crawled into the doorway of a small artist's gallery away from the nightlife and bedded down. The alcove was so dark that he had to turn his phone on to pull out his blanket. The battery was nearly dead. He located the handgun, just to make sure it was there, and then pulled out what remained of his cash. Holding it close to his face, he counted the tens and twenties, coming up with a total of six hundred thirty dollars, half of what he'd started with. Not bad, but not good either. Adan knew his money wouldn't last. Instead of buying food, he told himself he had to rely on handouts whenever he could find them. Weary of sleeping on the street, he told himself he'd try to get into a shelter in the morning. Many served breakfast. But that wouldn't solve the problem of dwindling resources. He needed a job.

Having turned his phone off and curled up under his blanket, his head resting on the duffel, his mind drifted away from the dark doorway and back to Whitehead with his table and chair on Royal Street. Of all the people he had met, he was the friendliest and most appealing. He hadn't tried to swindle him and he actually delivered on the goods. A man of his word. Adan was nervous about applying for a job, not having done it. Whitehead seemed free in offering advice. Adan thought of him as someone who enjoyed talking. Perhaps he could give him a few pointers, maybe he would know who was hiring. Maybe he was hiring.

29

Cornel Whitehead saw Adan coming down the sidewalk, his duffel strapped across his shoulder, looking just as homeless as he had the previous day and wearing the same clothes. It was early enough in the morning that the tourists had yet to hit the streets. The big man was preoccupied, scouting for a place to set up his wares, and at first paid him no attention when Adan approached.

"Hi, Cornel, it's me, Adan."

"I hear ya. What do you want?"

"Just thought I'd say hello. I saw you down the block."

Whitehead shook his head and faced Adan.

"So, what is it you want? You want to buy a fetish, I got a bunch of them."

"No, nothing like that. I thought, maybe, you could give me some advice."

"Advice? Look, just because we done business don't mean I'm your friend."

Adan felt deflated.

"I know that," Adan insisted. "I was just wondering if

you knew where I could get a job. People say you're an entrepreneur."

"On-tre-pre-noor," Whitehead said slowly. "Learn to pronounce the word before you try to use it."

"Sorry. On-tre-pre-noor," Adan said slowly.

"That's better. Now, I don't know what your problem is and I don't want to know. But a white boy like you should be able to find a job, no problem."

"You don't have any jobs?"

Whitehead laughed.

"I am my only employee. Was a time when I employed others but they'd steal from me or not show up so I refocused my business, so to speak, into a one-man operation. Besides, what do you know about selling?"

"Nothing," Adan admitted. "But I'm willing to learn."

"You got any work experience?"

"Sure," Adan lied.

"Where?"

"In Texas."

Whitehead rolled his eyes.

"What kind of business?" he said, annoyed.

"Oh. At a grocery store and places like that. Just part-time."

"Well, I'm not running a grocery store and I don't need help."

Cornel saw the effect of his words on Adan's face, which had gone from cheerfulness to gloom.

"Guy like you, homeless, no skills and with a fake ID for whatever reason. You got no place to start except the bottom. Maybe a dishwasher in some dive or chain restaurant."

"There's a lot of restaurants."

"Yeah, but you ain't getting a job at no Commander's Palace. You need to aim low."

Adan looked at Cornel blankly.

"It's a restaurant. One of the best in the city, and that's sayin' something."

"How low?"

"I already told you. But what am I saying? You don't listen to what I say anyway."

"How's that?"

"I tole you when we first met that you needed to bathe. Well, you still need to bathe. Or get yourself deodorant. Nobody's gonna hire a stink factory like you. Shower, shave, put on some clean clothes and then go look for places that are hiring."

"So, you don't know any place that's hiring?"

Cornel shook his head.

"You ain't listening."

Adan adjusted the strap of his duffel and watched Cornel as he eyed vendors down the street who were setting up tables.

"Why don't you just set up there?" Adan pointed.

"Don't have a permit. Besides, the guys with permits would chase me away."

"Why not get a permit?"

"Used to have one but I'm not the type of person who likes to sit in the same place all day. Sometimes the business is better elsewhere, though there are times that a permit might not be a bad idea."

Adan smiled weakly.

"Good luck, Cornel. I won't bother you no more."

"Look, there's a place opened a while back and they might be hiring. Coupla white gals from Minnesota or some godforsaken place decided Nawlins needed another restaurant. Could be outta business by now. It's off Magazine near Fourcher, if I remember correctly. Anyway, plenty of restaurants on Magazine. Maybe one of them is hiring."

30

As the new guy at the Chez Wally—the name an inside joke, Wally standing for walleye—Adan, or Justin Baker, as he wrote on his application, took his job seriously and washed dishes and bused tables for whatever hours he could get. The restaurant was located in what had once been someone's two-story house. The kitchen was in the back on the first floor. The front half consisted of a half-dozen tables with an additional serving area upstairs. It was not a good arrangement for anyone, especially the servers and busboys who had to carry heavy trays up and down the stairs. Turnover was high.

For Adan, the job represented another step away from his past. In addition to being paid minimum wage, he struck up conversations with other employees, especially Noah Scott, the dishwasher-busboy who had been working at Chez Wally since it opened. Older than Adan at twenty-five, a transplant from East Moline Correctional Center, where he'd spent a year rehabilitating following several convictions on drug charges, he shared a house with three young men who, like himself, had hit some kind of bottom.

The two worked different shifts and at first only saw each other coming and going.

Adan tried to take Cornel's advice before applying. He'd hiked to the Salvation Army shelter only to find that it had already filled up but got a free takeaway supper for his troubles. He saw a sign prohibiting weapons and realized he couldn't have spent the night there anyway. A steady rain that began shortly after he left the shelter slowed his progress as he sought a dry place to spend the night, settling for a spot among dozens of homeless under the Pontchartrain Expressway, some of them in tents. It was the best night's sleep he'd had in weeks.

Rising near sunrise, he hiked to Woldenberg Park on the river front and decided he would either hide the gun or toss it into the drink. It all depended on how nervous he got. Although he felt that he stuck out like a wanted poster, joggers paid him little attention as they passed by. Just another homeless guy on a bench. Across the walkway was a narrow band of grass met by a rocky slope that descended into the still water. He stuffed the plastic bags containing the pistol into his pants pocket and, leaving his duffel behind, moved to the embankment where he seated himself uncomfortably on a large rock and gazed momentarily at the river's sun splashed surface. With one last glance around him, he transferred the gun from his pocket, pushing it under a pile of smaller stones until his hand was buried up to the wrist. Rising, he smoothed out the small stones with his shoe and left the park with his duffel, making note of landmarks so that he could find the spot again.

Having secured a cot for the night, Adan showered and picked out a white shirt and black pants at a second hand store and the next morning headed to Chez Wally looking like a teenager with a bad haircut.

After his first week, the shelter charged ten dollars a night but the breakfast remained free. He learned quickly that nobody at the restaurant cared if he ate food that patrons hadn't finished, or in some cases, hadn't even touched. His first check was waiting for him Friday afternoon, his second week on the job. It was preprinted and embossed and looked official. It was the slow time after lunch and he visited with Noah, who had also received his check. Both men were in good moods.

"Got my first pay check," Adan said cheerfully. "Did you get yours?"

"Of course I got mine," Noah said. "Ain't no big deal. So, got any plans to celebrate?"

"Gotta work tonight."

"I mean after hours. You know, go out, have a few drinks."

"I would 'cept where I'm staying has a curfew if I'm not working."

"Let me guess, you're staying at a shelter."

Adan nodded sheepishly.

"How much you paying?"

"Ten bucks a night. But I can't stay there forever. I think there's a month limit, something like that. I'll have to check it out. Don't want to get thrown on the street from a homeless shelter."

"I hear that. Hey, Justin, don't worry. I stayed in a shelter too when I first got here. Nothin' to be ashamed about. The thing is not that you're in a shelter but what you're doing to get out."

Adan smiled. He was still getting used to being called by his new name, which he didn't like. He didn't see himself as a Justin.

"You know, at ten bucks a night, that's like three hundred for a month, even if you don't get kicked out."

"So? It beats sleeping under a bridge."

"Just so happens that one of my roomies is moving out this weekend. I got a two-bedroom place, fits four guys. You seem like a good guy. Rent's two-fifty a month and you'd share a bedroom."

"Hmmm."

"It's a good deal, man. Place ain't far and it's pretty safe. The other guys all work and it ain't a party house or nothing like that. 'Course, you gotta work it out with your roommate if you bring a girl up. But, you know, ain't no problem. We're pretty accommodating about women."

"Do I gotta sign anything, like a lease or something?"

"No. It's in my name. You'd be subleasing from me so there's nothing to sign. Whatayousay?"

Adan held out his fist.

"Good deal, man. You can move in Monday."

31

ADAN WAS RELIEVED TO FINALLY GET OFF THE STREETS, and when Monday morning came he could barely contain his excitement as he made his way from what he hoped was his last night in a shelter and toward the next step of his new life. Noah Scott was not nearly as enthusiastic when he answered Adan's persistent knocking.

"Man," he said, wearing only undershorts, "you're early."

"You didn't say when I should come over," Adan said, surprised that Noah's muscular upper body was covered with tattoos, a mix of Nazi and white power expressions and symbols.

"My bad," Noah said. "I was out late last night. Kinda hung over. Didn't mean to, but sometimes it just works out that way. Why don'tcha come in. What time is it?"

"'Bout eight or so," Adan said, dropping his duffel in the narrow entry.

"That all you got?"

"Yep. Just me and my bag."

"Well, the place is furnished so you don't need anything anyway."

The single-story shotgun house was situated on a narrow lot. The three-step porch had lost its paint eons ago and the house itself had once been painted either blue or gray but now was largely unpainted clapboard siding. Air conditioners stuck out of several windows in the narrow corridors separating adjacent houses. Rusting chainlink fencing marked the property lines. The small backyard included a dilapidated shed and an unfinished brick patio. Islands of weeds struggled to survive here and there. The asphalt roof had a dip along one side, as if the interior supporting members had partially collapsed.

"Your room is on the right in the back," Noah said sleepily as Adan followed him into the large, spare kitchen, where he brewed coffee using a French press. "The roommates are already gone."

Adan took a seat at the kitchen table and took everything in. It was not so far removed from his grandfather's house. The cabinets were site built with ill-fitting plywood doors, chipped around the edges. The doors were painted gold and the frames black—Saints colors.

"We share the fridge," Noah said, setting two steaming coffee mugs on the table. Adan nodded as he took his first sip.

"This is hot," Adan said, spitting some of brew into the cup.

"S'posed to be. You can get an ice cube outta the fridge if you want."

Adan smiled.

"So, I can put stuff in the fridge?"

Noah gave him a puzzled look.

"'Course you can. Didn't you hear what I said?"

"Just want to make sure. I've never shared a place before."

"Lucky you. You're on your own when it comes to eatin'. Once in a while we'll do a barbecue in the back but mostly you eat what you bring. Same goes for drinkin', comin' and going. Mostly, we share the rent and utilities. Even if you don't run your A/C, you pay a quarter of the utilities so if you think you can save money by sweatin', don't bother. That reminds me, you got the rent money?"

Adan nodded.

"It's in my bag."

"Well, go get it," Noah said following a momentary pause. "Just the money, not the bag."

Adan dragged his duffel into the kitchen.

"I just said not to bring the bag in here. Are you not listening?"

"Sorry. I'm kinda excited, you know, getting off the street and all," Adan said apologetically, as he dug into the olive green bag, finally coming up with his cash. Even though the wad had shrunk considerably, it looked like a lot of money when he set it on the table. Noah grinned.

Adan counted out currency and handed the rent money to Noah as he double wrapped the blue rubber band around the remainder of his funds. Noah had watched as Adan counted it out and laid the stack of bills in front of him.

"Don't put it away yet," Noah said. "I need another two fifty for the deposit."

Adan's smile vanished like smoke.

"Deposit for what?" he asked, suspiciously.

"You ain't never rented before?"

"I just stayed with people."

"Well, the landlord charged me a deposit and so anyone stays in the house owes me a deposit, you know, to cover damages and such. Don't worry, you'll get it back when you leave, assuming you don't skip out. I been here two years and so far I've had, what, five roommates."

"What about the guy who moved out this time?"

"Oh, he got caught shoplifting for the umpteenth time and he's at the parish jail doing six months. He's was hopin' to stay free but the judge didn't see it that way. No big deal. Happens to a lot of folks."

"You, too?"

"Yeah, me, too."

32

Adan's room consisted of a pair of single beds, a small, wood student's desk with chair, two small wood dressers, one a glossy red, the other stained to look like walnut. An armoire served as a closet. A small air conditioner filled the lower half of a window with a view of an adjacent house.

"The red one's yours," Noah said.

Adan pulled the top drawer open. It was stuffed with clothing.

"That was Dan's dresser. You can put his stuff in a garbage bag or a box or whatever. I'll put it in the attic in case he comes back, which I doubt."

"Where's the bags?"

"They're in the kitchen. Forgot to tell you, we put ten dollars into a kitty every month to buy stuff like garbage bags, soap, stuff like that that everybody can use. I don't know about you, but I'm hungry. Gonna scrounge somethin' up for breakfast. You good?"

"Yeah, I had breakfast at the shelter."

Adan sat on the edge of his bed as Noah left. The room was about the size of his room in his grandfather's house, only he'd had a closet and a ceiling fan instead of an air conditioner. The relief he'd felt earlier in the morning had largely abated after the unexpected expense of a deposit. He wondered whether it would have mattered had Noah told him about it beforehand. He couldn't see himself as a homeless person moving from shelter to shelter, existing on handouts and getting nowhere. Still, the two hundred fifty dollar deposit hurt. He had less than three hundred dollars left, including the money from work, and he vowed to make every dollar count as he did the math in his head. Forty hours a week at minimum wage gave him a little less than two hundred dollars after the Social Security deduction. He didn't earn enough to have taxes deducted, the only bright spot on the earnings front.

He wasn't bothered at being at the bottom of the economic ladder. He didn't think of it that way. He'd been brought up at the bottom of the ladder and for most of his life assumed that was just the way things were. Some people had money and some people didn't. Some people got screwed and some people didn't. Wasn't about what you deserved, his grandfather believed.

"People call us white trash," Harley had told him more than once. "These people, they ain't no better than us. They don't call us names to our faces. They hide behind their money."

And then the old man would fly off into one of his drunken rages against minorities, as if in a town that was ninety-five percent white, blacks and Hispanics had somehow stolen jobs and opportunity from him. And when he was done complaining about minorities he lashed out at the government and its system of squeezing whatever surplus a poor man had through the subterfuge of taxation.

Adan wasn't sure if he believed any of it or all of it. He questioned a lot of things his grandfather said, but so far in his seventeen years he had no reason to dismiss it.

33

ADAN HADN'T EXPECTED TO FIND ANYTHING USEFUL IN the chest of drawers. The clothing fit someone much taller than him and looked to be in good shape, as if purchased new. One of the drawers was filled with cell phones, several wallets, keys, pocket knives, credit cards, money clips and a half-empty box of firecrackers. The bottom was covered with coins of various denominations. It was a junk drawer of small treasures.

He spent a half hour going through the contents, opening each wallet, some of which contained identification but no currency. Most of the wallets belonged to people from out of state. He wondered whether these were the kind of possessions someone would want to keep. The coins didn't amount to much more than five dollars and the SIM cards had been removed from most of the phones. Given that the owner was in jail, Adan assumed this was his stash of stolen items.

"Hey, Noah," Adan said as he entered the kitchen. Noah wasn't there.

The sound of clanging metal erupted somewhere in the

back of the house and, as Adan moved toward it, he saw through the back screen door Noah lying on a weight bench pushing a barbell. Adan watched from the inside, waiting for a break in his workout before interrupting.

"I see you," Noah said, still pumping iron. "What up?"

"I found some stuff in one of the drawers."

"You mean the phones and stuff?" Noah said, coming to a sitting position, his legs straddling the bench.

"Yeah. Lots of weird stuff."

"Dan sometimes rolled drunks, usually guys who were in town to raise hell but caught hell instead. Police don't spend a lotta time on tourists who put themselves in stupid situations unless they get on the news. They prolly won't come back anyway. It ain't called the Big Easy for nothing."

"What should I do with it?"

"You checked it out already?"

"Yeah, shouldn't I?"

"That's fine."

"Is he gonna come back for this stuff? I mean, the phones don't have SIM cards and—"

"He might come back, but he won't be able to stay here unless there's a vacancy. He knows that."

"It's pretty heavy with the phones and the coins."

"You can keep the money. He won't care about the phones. He already sold the SIM cards. And he was too afraid to use the credit cards. You can try 'em if you want, though I'd think they've been deactivated."

"Yeah, I don't know nothin' about that. I'll keep the coins and toss the phones and put the rest in the trash bag with his clothes."

"Sure, why not?" Noah said, returning to his workout. "One other thing, don't interrupt my workout. Wait till I'm finished next time."

Adan pulled the drawer out of the chest, pocketed the coins, which made his pants bulge, dropped the phones into the kitchen trash can, stacked the credit cards on the top of the chest and dumped everything else into the bag containing Dan's clothing. The bottom drawer was filled with Mardi Gras beads, face masks and trinkets. Although he was aware of Mardi Gras, he had no idea why anyone would collect the beads, much less why anyone would wear them.

Dipping his hands into the colorful collection, he felt something hard concealed under the beads.

"I'll be damned," he said, lifting a laptop computer, holding it close to his face like an etching.

34

IN CONTRAST TO THE BEDROOMS, WHICH WERE AS unkempt as would be expected of young men, the living room was pristine and filled with electronics, including a sixty-inch wall-mounted 4K TV, Xbox and PlayStation. A box on the coffee table overflowed with controllers and accessories. The wall opposite the TV was draped with a large Confederate battle flag. Furnishings were from Ikea, including a leather sofa pushed against the wall beneath the flag and several Poang chairs in black leather and a small book case stuffed with video games and DVDs.

Everyone in the house had a laptop, pads, smartphones, the works. His roommate, Jeremy Walker, helped him set up the laptop he'd inherited from the previous roommate. When Jeremy wasn't earning a living as an Uber driver, he was at the house working out on the Xbox. At twenty-two, he had a vague notion of going pro one day, though he mostly played against Zach Jacobs, Noah's roommate, who enjoyed video games but lacked Jeremy's dexterity and intensity. In addition to smoking marijuana, Jeremy enjoyed the occasional oxycodone tablet, which he took secretly because Noah's house rules banned opiates.

"I only do it once in a while," Jeremy told Adan. "I'm not addicted to it, though I can see why some people are. Ever try it?"

"Nope. Just weed."

"Well, if you ever want to, let me know. I'm not sayin' you should but, you know, you get curious about it I can get you a 10 mil tab. Don't tell Noah, he's got a thing about this shit. Doesn't want it around. So, like, this is just between you and me. You right with that?"

Adan nodded and watched impatiently as Jeremy reconfigured the laptop, finally handing it to him after entering the password for the house's wi-fi.

"You know much about computers?" Jeremy asked.

"Just from using them at school. I'm not a nerd or anything like that."

"Just so you know, don't ever tell anybody the password. Nobody. Got that?" Jeremy said gravely. "You run into any problems with your laptop just tell me and I'll help. The other thing, you know better than to open emails from strangers and that sort of thing. Right?"

"Well, yeah," Adan said, not looking up from the screen. "'Course, I don't get many emails. I mean all I had was an account at school so—"

"We'll set you up. I'll talk to Noah about it. He's the boss here but I'm sure it'll be OK."

"So, can I use it? Like for surfing?"

"Have at it."

As Jeremy left the room, Adan smiled, sitting at the desk, eager to learn what he could about his crime.

35

ADAN FOUND A NEW FRIEND IN HIS LAPTOP. WHEN HE wasn't at work, he was sitting at his desk surfing the net. He'd learned that the news stories about his crime had diminished quickly. The initial stories in the Beaumont media seemed to have been picked up by every news outlet in the region and then dropped out of sight. He felt good about that. The crime, or rather his status as a fugitive, was uppermost in his mind. Early on, he felt that everyone he met knew what he had done even though they were complete strangers and probably hadn't heard of Vidor. He learned from surfing that he was suffering from consciousness of guilt. He knew he'd committed the crime and according to his own value system he should have taken responsibility. But knowing this and acting on it were two different things. As much as he struggled with his sense of guilt, he didn't want to jeopardize his freedom, and the longer ago that it had happened, the less connection he felt, as if one day it would no longer feel real to him, as if it hadn't actually happened.

The second weekend at the house was something of a

coming out party for Adan. He'd become accustomed to his roommates, who knew him as Justin Baker, but wasn't certain how far he could trust them, nor they him. Another thing he learned while surfing was that Crime Stoppers had put a reward of two thousand five hundred dollars on him. It included a photo from his student ID depicting a boyish looking teen with long hair. Thinking about it made him feel vulnerable, as if anyone he met could turn him in. He didn't like misleading his roommates, especially Noah, who had taken him in, and Jeremy, who had proven to be helpful. Zach wasn't around as much during the day and since Adan worked at night they saw each other mostly on the weekend.

The four of them were in the living room watching college football games with the sound off, switching channels whenever a commercial came on. None of them were native Louisianians. Noah had embraced the city, had lived there the longest even though he seemed to have the shittiest job. Adan wondered about that. He also wondered how Jeremy could afford a Prius by simply driving for Uber.

"Noah didn't tell you, huh," Jeremy said, stifling a cough after passing a joint to Zach.

"We're thieves," Zach said proudly, sucking on the joint.

"You see all this stuff we got? Most of it ain't ours, or wasn't until we stole it."

"That's what we do," Zach agreed, grinning.

"We all have jobs so we have income sources. People pick up on stuff. They see you with a lot of electronics and no visible means of support, well, that ain't good," Noah said.

"Yeah. It'd be like if you dealt drugs and people drove up to your house twenty times a day. Neighbors would get suspicious," Jeremy said. "So what we got nice stuff? We got jobs. End of story."

"Wow, I never would've guessed it," Adan said.

Zach and Jeremy exchanged glances.

"That's good," Zach said, smiling. "That's how we want it. But, you know, you ain't told us much about yourself."

"I told you I'm from Texas."

"Yeah," Noah said. "But you lied about your name."

"What?"

"I looked at your wallet and your crappy ID. That ain't real," Zach said coldly.

"It isn't?"

"Don't act stupid," Noah said. "We're not gonna do anything. We just want you to be honest about it, like starting with your fucking name."

Adan groaned resignedly.

"My name's Adan Burke."

"And—"

"And I shot a kid in Vidor and I'm on the run."

"Holy shit!" Jeremy exclaimed.

36

NONE OF ADAN'S ROOMMATES HAD ACTUALLY BEEN A fugitive. No reward had been offered for their capture. No one had been looking for them when they were caught. None of them had shot anyone. Noah had spent a year in a medium-security prison in Illinois for a drug bust, his second. Zach had served time in Indiana for burglary, and Jeremy had been collared in Oklahoma for identity theft and credit card abuse. But that was just the surface.

As Adan described what had happened and how much he regretted it, the others let down their shields. Though he hadn't joined a gang, Noah had bulked up in prison and turned much of his body into a canvas of creepy racist and anti-authoritarian art.

"Now that you brought it up," Jeremy said, "I'm a parole violator."

"What?" Noah exclaimed. "You violated?"

"Yeah," Jeremy said, sheepishly, his eyes cast downward.

"And you're just telling us now?"

"Yeah, well, I thought if I told you, you wouldn't let me live here."

Noah shook his head, sighing.

"They're not looking for me."

"How do you know?"

"Look, it was a nonviolent crime. I did my time. I just wanted to get out of Oklahoma, you know, start over."

"It's just that, you know, it would've been nice. I even asked you."

"No you didn't," Jeremy said, defensively. "But I would've lied if you did. Just look at you. You're pissed now that I told you."

"I'm not pissed," Noah said.

"I'm sure you haven't told us everything. But it's your house. You make the rules. You want me to go, I'll go," Jeremy said resentfully.

"No. I don't want you to go," Noah said emphatically. "We got a good thing going here. Who wants to screw with that?"

Zach smiled, giving fist bumps to Noah and Jeremy. Looking critically at Adan, who sat stiffly on the sofa, he asked, slyly, "What did you do with the gun?"

All eyes were on Adan as he shifted his weight, leaning forward, folding his hands between his knees.

"I hid it."

"You still got it?" Noah asked.

"Yeah. I wasn't sure what to do with it so I kept it."

Noah suddenly rose from his chair, alarmed.

"Is it in the house?"

"No. I don't have it with me. I hid it."

His roommates seemed confounded when he described where he'd buried it. None of them had ever committed a gun crime but they were curious. They asked him about the gun, how many shots he'd fired, whether he'd used it in other crimes and finally, whether they could see it.

"You guys don't believe me?"

"No, we believe you," Noah said. "It's just that, Christ, I don't know. In a way I want to see it and in another way I don't. Weird, huh?"

"Maybe you and him can fetch it," Zach suggested.

"I don't know about that," Jeremy said cautiously.

"What's the harm?" Zach argued. "We can always get rid of it. Right, Adan?"

"Sure, whatever. The only reason I didn't throw it away was 'cause I didn't know if I'd need it. It belonged to my gramps."

"You stole it from your own grandpa?"

"I didn't steal it. I just took it to school. I thought it wasn't loaded."

"Famous last words," Zach said, smiling.

37

"I don't like this at all," Noah insisted after Adan and Jeremy left.

"You mean the gun?"

"The whole thing. The gun, sure, but if I'd known the cops were looking for him he wouldn't be living here. I don't like the idea of harboring a fugitive. And Jeremy violating. That was news to me."

"Would you have rented to Jeremy if you'd known?"

"I don't know."

"Could be all the people you've been renting to were hiding something like that and you didn't know it."

"But now I do," Noah said. "What about you? You hiding something?"

"Me? No, why would you say that?"

"Just asking."

"So, are you gonna kick him out?"

"Fuck if I know."

"He sure as hell ain't gonna go to the cops if you throw him out."

Exhaling slowly, sitting in his Poang, his eyes on the

silent TV, thoughts racing, Noah thought he'd been careful in vetting roommates, but his focus was less on their past and more on the present. No serious druggies. No assholes. Young men who could handle shady business. At first, he wanted to make it honestly but he realized quickly that wasn't likely to happen with his record. Having been released from a state prison on a state felony was a big deal with employers. So he learned how to make his way with an honest job and a dishonest sideline. Theft and burglary was as far as he wanted to go. And it not only helped ends meet, but put money in the bank. But he worried about what Griswold would think if he found out. Actually, he knew what he would think. And it wasn't good.

38

JEREMY PARKED IN A LOT OVERLOOKING THE RIVER behind and above the Cafe Du Monde and followed Adan as he led him to the bench where he'd sat while deciding what to do with the gun. The two sat there in silence for several minutes.

"What are we waiting for?" Jeremy asked. "Is this the right place?"

Adan nodded.

"So, where is it?"

"It's over there, under those rocks on the other side of the sidewalk," pointing with his head.

"So, what are you waiting for?"

"Just wanna make sure nobody's watching."

"That's impossible," Jeremy said. "This is New Orleans. Somebody's always watching."

"I mean, like a cop."

"Oh, yeah."

Jeremy swiveled his head to the left and right and then awkwardly behind him.

"There's some tourists up there looking at the river. I wouldn't worry about them. Why don'cha get it right now."

Adan eyed the rocky embankment nervously. He wondered if the gun was still there. It wouldn't have bothered him if someone had taken it, except for the fact it could be traced to his grandfather. He resented Jeremy's pushiness, as if he were egging him on into something he'd soon regret. He thought about how odd it would be for someone to just go down to the embankment and start digging through the rocks. He'd buried it deep enough so that if someone lifted the top rock, the gun would remain hidden.

"Just go down there and tie your shoe or something," Jeremy urged. "It's no big thang."

"Easy for you to say."

"Look, if I knew where it was I'd get it."

"OK, OK," Adan said, anxiously.

Staring at his shoes, he untied one of the laces and, rising slowly from the bench, he approached the embankment, hovering over the area where he'd deposited the gun, glancing down at his feet and in an exaggerated way kneeling to tie his shoe, within reach of his target. Looking up and down the walkway, he inched closer to the rocks and slowly pushed aside the topmost stones, his respiration quickening as he failed to immediately locate the weapon. He couldn't tell whether time seemed to have slowed down or speeded up, but anxiety had overtaken him like a hangover. Feeling exposed, he fumbled to retie his shoe when a shadow fell over him.

"What the fuck," Jeremy whispered crossly. "What's takin' you?"

"I can't find it," Adan whispered apprehensively, still working on his shoe.

"Goddamn it," Jeremy said, leaning over Adan, burying his hand under the stones. "Are you sure this is the place?"

"Yeah. I remember where the bench was and—"

"I found it," Jeremy said excitedly, grabbing the gun, wrapped in its plastic bags, instantly shoving it into his pants pocket, straightening himself and moving away from Adan, who pushed himself off the walkway, his shoe tied, his heart racing.

"I'm glad it's a small gun," Jeremy said as they returned to his car. "Is it loaded?"

"Yeah, it's loaded."

39

Once in the car, Jeremy handed the gun to Adan and then phoned Noah.

"He wants us to meet him at the storage unit," Jeremy said after ending the brief conversation.

"The storage unit?"

"Yeah, it's where we keep our stuff."

They drove over the Crescent City Connection to a place in Gretna. Adan felt excited as he crossed the river for the first time, marveling at how high they were.

"This useta be a toll bridge," Jeremy said.

"You sure can see a lot," Adan said as he twisted his body to get a panoramic view.

Noah and Zach were waiting for them as they parked. Noah led them around the side of the converted warehouse to a hallway providing interior access to the storage unit, which was the size of a one-car garage.

"This is where we keep everything," Noah told Adan.

The walls were lined with heavy-duty metal shelves, with a row of shelving down the middle. The shelves contained laptops and pads, video games and players, memory cards, cell phones, flat-screen TVs and tools. Several high-end bicycles were positioned in a corner. Before Adan could say anything, Noah held out his hand. Not knowing what he meant by it, Adan shook Noah's hand.

"Gimme the gun," Noah said, annoyed.

Noah removed the clip, checked the chamber and placed it in the back of a shelf, wrapped in the bag.

"The only reason I'm keeping it is because I'm not sure what to do with it," he told Adan while the others watched. "We don't keep guns in the house and you may notice we don't have guns here either. We don't mess with them. They're nothing but trouble for guys like us."

"We sometimes find guns," Zach said, "and we got someone who pays us for 'em and he does whatever with them."

"So, what're you gonna do with my gun?"

"I just told you," Noah said. "I don't know. Yet."

"If you sell it to someone, you know, it'll be traced back to my gramps and he could get into trouble."

"From what you told us, you shoulda thought about that before you shot that kid," Noah said, harshly.

Adan frowned and distracted himself by scanning the goodies on the shelves.

"I don't mean to be an asshole," Noah said, "but I don't know what to do with your gun or with you, you want the truth."

This wasn't the first time someone had something similar to him. His grandfather had said similar things to him so many times that Adan paid it no attention. But it chafed, coming from a person he considered to be a friend.

"I didn't know what to do with it either," Adan said in his defense. "I shouldn't have told y'all about it."

"It ain't just the gun," Noah said with a hint of exasperation. "It's the fucking ... you didn't—"

"You didn't tell us you was a fugitive," Zach said.

Jeremy had been quiet until now.

"Yeah, you really shoulda told us."

Noah glared at Jeremy.

"You're no better, man," Noah said sharply. "You didn't tell us you violated. Fuck, here we are driving around and we get stopped for running a stop sign and we all go to jail for harboring."

Jeremy lowered his head sheepishly.

"I'm sorry, man. I asked if I could move out of state for a job but my probation officer wouldn't even try. He was such a jerk."

"Let's just drop it for now," Noah said. "We're not going to settle anything here."

40

"I DON'T KNOW WHAT THE FUCK TO DO," NOAH confessed to Zach as they drove back to the house. "I've never been in this situation."

"Me either. But, you know, Jeremy's been good. And Adan's got that false ID. He says he's never been finger-printed. How the cops gonna know who he is?"

"I s'pose."

"You were lucky you got released, man."

"Yeah, I know. Clean living in the joint and the state running outta money. I couldn't believe Jeremy. Man."

"Yeah, but his rap was like fraud. Small time shit. Who's gonna pay to look for him? It's not like he's a bail jumper where there's money involved."

"So I oughta just forget about it?"

Sitting at a stoplight, Zach watched pedestrians crossing and, glancing at his rear view mirror, he noticed a police car several cars behind them. Putting both hands on the wheel of the van, one eye on the rear view, he pulled away slowly when the light changed. By the time they'd reached the next light, the police car was directly behind them.

"Don't look now," he whispered, "but the cops are behind us."

"Why do you say things like that?" Noah said, resisting the urge to look back.

"Well, it's true."

"Yeah, but what am I s'posed to do about it?"

"I'm nervous, I guess."

"Well, you ain't doin' nothing wrong."

"I just don't like it, man. I get the willies every time I see a cop car."

"Well, don't do anything stupid."

With Zach focusing on his driving, they drove to the next traffic light, the police car still following. Then he felt his phone vibrate followed by a distinctive tone.

"Shit," he said. "That's my boss. Fuck. I can't answer with the cops behind us."

Seeing his friend's agitation, Noah suggested they make a turn, which they did at the next opportunity.

"Well, that's a relief. They're not following us," Zach said, looking at his phone as he drove. "I'll drop you off at the house. I gotta go to work."

"Whatever."

41

ADAN WASN'T SURE WHAT TO THINK. HE HADN'T expected Noah to react the way he did about his status as a fugitive. He wasn't as obsessed about it as he had been. He wasn't looking over his shoulder every minute, wasn't living in constant fear of discovery. He was just a teenager trying to figure out where his life was going. He'd thought he found a friend but now he wasn't sure.

"Don't worry about it," Jeremy told him at the house as they talked in their room.

"But what if he throws me out?"

"He won't do that. It's not the best situation but it is what it is. Noah just needs to think about it. It'll work out."

Noah went straight to his weights in the back yard after Zach dropped him off, moving past Adan and Jeremy without saying a word. He needed to burn off energy. He was angry and frustrated and wanted to lash out but directed his fury into pumping iron. How much of a threat was Adan? he wondered between sets. Shooting a student at a school seemed like a big deal to him. He needed more information and between sets read as many stories on his phone as he could find. There was a lot of publicity initially. It seemed like every media outlet in Texas had something on it. And then it dropped from sight. But what could he do about it? He told himself he couldn't afford to let it fester. One way or another he had to deal with it, make a decision. Since it affected everyone in the house, he'd put it to a vote.

42

Noah wasted no time after Zach returned from work. The four assembled in the living room sans TV, grass and beer.

"Y'all know as much about Adan as I do and so you need to decide whether he stays or goes."

"We gonna vote him off the island?" Jeremy said.

"That's up to you."

"Why don't we just let him stay?" Jeremy said.

Noah sighed.

"Because, there's probably a fugitive task force looking for him and if he's caught here we all go to jail. See the problem?"

Zach eyed Adan suspiciously, who was sitting on the couch, his head down.

"It's hard to believe you shot someone," he said. "You don't look like the type."

"Leave him alone," Jeremy said. "We're not gonna hurt you."

Adan looked up momentarily, smiling grimly.

"Look, we just need to decide if it's worth the risk to let

him stay or not," Noah said sternly. "I already told you what the risk is."

"Yeah, but can't we say we thought he was someone else?" Zach said.

"Yeah, we didn't know his real name till he told us," Jeremy agreed.

"So, you're saying ignorance is an excuse?"

Jeremy and Zach looked at one another, each waiting for the other to respond.

"That's not what I'm saying," Zach said. "Look at that Bulger guy. He was a stone cold killer and it took years and years for the Feds to find him and he was hiding in plain sight. All the kid has to do is stay out of trouble and they'll never find him. My guess is that they don't even know he's in Louisiana. Besides, it's not like we're gonna spend the rest of our lives here. I'm not, that's for sure."

"What's wrong with being here?" Jeremy said.

"You know what I mean."

"Don't you have plans for the future?" Noah asked.

Jeremy shrugged.

"I like things the way they are. I like the Uber deal and havin' a lotta time to myself. And I like what we do. It's exciting."

"Not me. I like the excitement and I like you guys but I wanna get more into something legit and away from the shit we do," Zach said.

Noah nodded in agreement. He'd been watching Adan while they discussed his future. The teen hadn't reacted to anything, as if he'd either given up or didn't care.

"What do you think, Adan?" Noah asked. "What would you do if you were us?"

"I don't know. I'd rather not think about it."

"So you're fine with us thinking about it for you?"

"I guess. I feel bad about it. I just don't know what I can do."

"Grow some stones," Zach scolded. "That pisses me off. Tell us why we should let you stay."

"Maybe I should just leave. It'd save you guys the trouble of throwing me out."

The three of them looked at him with dismay. They thought they were throwing him a rope and instead of taking it he seemed to be pushing it away. Zach approached Adan and put his hands on his shoulders.

"Get up," he demanded. "Fuck man, give us a reason not to throw you out. Defend yourself, for chrissake."

"I can't," Adan said, looking up at Zach. "Maybe I should just turn myself in and get it over with. This is gonna follow me my whole life, ain't it?"

"It is what it is, man," Jeremy said. "But, why give up? Maybe we can get you better ID, teach you how we operate. But, you know, you'd have to become one of us."

"He could use some tats," Zach mused.

"And you gotta come clean with us," Noah said. "What else you holding back? You ain't nineteen like you said."

"I'll be eighteen in November and I was raised by my gramps."

"What happened to your parents?"

"I never met my mom and my dad's been in prison since I was eight."

43

ALTHOUGH NO FORMAL VOTE WAS TAKEN, ADAN remained at the house. He hadn't brought it up, but Noah feared that if Adan were back on the street and got picked up by the police he might narc on his roommates to get a lighter sentence. He was certain if the teen was caught he'd identify himself. His age and inexperience made him malleable and for the time being Noah thought he could use Adan to his advantage, though there was never any doubt in his mind that he would be better off had he never met the young man. There were too many possibilities to work through to make a decision, so things continued as they were. At least that's what he wanted everyone to think. No point in making everyone uneasy, especially since he hadn't worked out a solution.

The only person Noah could think of who might offer advice on what to do about Adan was Chester Griswold, the landlord. Griswold was old school in every way. Having served six years of a fifteen-year term for armed robbery, he'd spent the recent past converting a dilapidated former motel into a compound outside Metairie. Six-foot, two hundred twenty pounds, bald, heavily tatted, his joints aching from the ill effects of years of human growth hormone, he was Noah's go-to man for fencing items that couldn't be sold locally or online. Grizz had connections throughout Louisiana and could export stolen goods into Mexico and Central America, for a price. Suspicious by nature, his grasp of technology ended with untraceable cell phones. The one thing he regretted was not having found a way to get into cybercrime, which seemed to him to be risk free compared to hijacking delivery trucks. He'd tried but he didn't get along with the punks who practiced the craft. They were young, cocky and arrogant and didn't respect his fifty-two years. So, he got rid of them, stuck with what he knew.

Noah asked for a meeting, ostensibly to deliver the bicycles from the storage unit.

"What are they worth?" Grizz asked.

"One retails for nine thousand and the other for seventy five large."

"Condition?"

"Excellent. Never been ridden. Don't even have pedals. Think you can take them?"

"How much you want to get out of this?"

"How about eighteen hundred for both."

"How about fifteen hundred?"

Noah quickly agreed to the price and sent Jeremy and Adan to retrieve the bicycles using Noah's van. Adan directed Jeremy as he backed the van into the large, overhead bay in the center of the weathered building. The two loitered after loading the bikes. Adan examined the contents of the shelves while Jeremy toyed with Adan's handgun, pointing it at the teen.

"Hey, what're you doing?" Adan blurted, shielding himself with his hands.

"It's not loaded," Jeremy said, replacing it in its plastic bag.

"So, what's Noah going to do with the bikes?"

"Well, he's not gonna ride 'em."

"I'd ride 'em. They look like cool bikes."

"They're too hot to ride."

"Too hot?"

"Yeah. You know what they're worth?"

Adan shrugged.

"Thousands, man."

"Really. Thousands. I didn't know bikes could cost that much. And these don't even have pedals."

"Shit. There's bikes that cost fifty thou and more."

Adan shook his head in disbelief.

"These high end bikes are rare so somebody sees you riding they might get suspicious. They end up getting sold in South America or Mexico."

"Y'all go to Mexico?"

"Not us. Other guys. With connections. You know what fences are, right?"

"Yeah, they're the guys who sell stolen property."

"We better get going. We don't like to spend much time here. In and out."

"Don't want to attract attention, is that it?"

"You never want to attract attention, except for women. Then you want all the attention you can get."

44

For a time, things settled into a routine. Adan was put to work scanning obituaries on newspaper web sites. Some of them went into great detail about the interests of the deceased and some of those interests had profit written all over them. Survivors writing the obits often tried to make the deceased look more interesting in death than he or she was in life. One such remembrance mentioned in detail the decedent's extensive collection of vintage radios. Noah had instructed the teen to look for references to collections, especially precious metals and artwork. After a few web searches Adan was excited to learn that a vintage radio could be worth thousands.

The trick to stealing from the dead was to act quickly. Survivors, though they may have had their eyes on objects they would claim for themselves, often waited until after the funeral before going through their dead relative's belongings. Noah was skeptical when Adan approached him with what he'd learned.

"Sounds bulky and heavy," Noah said dismissively.

"You should check it out," Adan said. "These are radios

that you put on a table, not the big ones. I can get some printouts for you."

While Adan sent several screens to a printer, Noah asked Zach what he thought.

"Never heard of it. I kinda thought radios went the way of the dinosaur."

"Yeah, but dinosaur bones are worth a lot," Noah mused.

Paging through the printouts, Noah's eyes widened.

"He's on to something here," Noah said, handing the printouts to Zach.

"Look at this one," Zach said, holding up a printout. "Two thousand dollars. I had no idea."

Standing in front of Noah in the living room, Adan beamed with excitement. He felt like he was contributing to the crew.

"But how do we know what this guy's got?" Noah asked, as Adan took a seat.

"The obituary said he was a lifelong collector," Adan said. "I'll get it for you."

After reading the printout of the obituary, Noah and Zach grinned. The deceased wasn't married and didn't have children. His survivors were siblings and their offspring. The only personal reference to him was that he'd been a lifelong collector of vintage radios.

"How do we sell this stuff?" Zach asked.

"Like anything else, I guess," Noah said. "Craigslist, online. Where's this guy live? We should check out his house."

Zach was online with his laptop and had the address within minutes.

"It's off Mirabeau in Gentilly."

45

THE DECEASED RADIO COLLECTOR HAD MADE IT EASY for Noah's crew. Each radio was meticulously labeled with its vintage, condition and price. They were arranged on shelving in a back room of the pastel blue folk Victorian with a front bay window and wraparound porch. A narrow driveway led from the street to the back of the house, where they parked the van. The family had placed a generic For Sale sign on the front lawn. Noah had instructed them to take the most valuable table top radios. There were at least sixty radios, some of them duplicates. They were arranged one in front of another in as many as three rows.

"Make sure you put something in place of the ones we take," Noah instructed them. "We don't want it to look like anything's missing. I'll bet none of the relatives knows anything about radios. They'll be happy to get what they can for what's left."

Although it was difficult to resist the temptation to take all of the most valuable radios, he made sure they left several expensive units on the shelves.

"The guy was a collector," he told them. "He wouldn't

just be collecting crap. And be careful when you put them in the van. We don't want to break anything."

They were in and out in thirty minutes, having collected two dozen tube radios, mostly Catalins and Bakelites from the nineteen thirties and forties.

"That was a great op," Noah said encouragingly, as they made space in the storage unit for their new acquisitions. "No fuss, no muss."

"I'll bet they'll never know what they're missing," Zach said.

"You see how quick they put up the For Sale sign," Jeremy said. "I mean the guy isn't buried yet."

"Yeah, they're just looking to cash out as quick as they can. They'll look at the tags and see dollar signs and they won't wonder whether anything's missing," Noah said.

Adan, whose idea it was to steal the radios, quietly admired the pristine radios lined up at chest height across several shelving units, touching them gently, turning dials and knobs, imagining what they sounded like.

"Good job, Adan," Noah said, patting him on the shoulder. "Grand total for the radios, according to the tags, is over twenty thousand dollars. Can you believe it?"

"That's a lot, huh?"

"A lot? Damn, that's the best haul we've ever had," Noah said enthusiastically. "By far."

"That's sick, man," Jeremy agreed.

"Now all we gotta do is figure out how to get top dollar for 'em," Zach said.

"I'm gonna leave that up to Adan here," Noah said. "Can you handle it?"

"I'll try," Adan nodded, grinning sheepishly.

46

"WE NEED TO GET YOU SOME TATS," JEREMY SAID, sipping a beer while Adan worked the web on his laptop to determine how to sell the radios. "White power tats. Whaddya think about that?"

Adan shrugged, focused on his task.

"You believe in white power, right?" Jeremy asked uncertainly. "You're not one of those liberals, right?"

"I guess," Adan said, turning in his chair to face Jeremy, who sat on the edge of his single bed.

"You guess what? That you're a liberal?"

"No," Adan said dismissively. "I don't pay much attention to that stuff."

"So, you believe in white nationalism then?"

"Not sure what it is."

"Well, it's where you put your race ahead of the other races. You know, you don't like the other races, like the nigs and beaners and slants and Jews, but you're OK with them if they stay outta your business, you know, the white race's business."

"I guess. I mean, the only black guy I've talked to was

the guy I got my ID from here in New Orleans. There weren't any blacks where I'm from."

"Sounds like a great place."

"I don't know. People called us white trash, white people called us white trash."

"Well, that ain't right. White people need to band together, defend themselves against the other races if it comes down to it."

"Shoot, they'd put us in jail if they could," Adan said bitterly. "That's what they did to my dad and all he did was defend himself against a guy who attacked him. I didn't know much about it 'cause it happened when I was little, but when I start to think about it I get pissed off. It wasn't fair, no way."

"I know what you mean. That's how it happens. You got white people who treat their own kind like niggers. They're traitors to their own race."

"They're the ones I really hate," Adan said. "The ones that put my dad in jail on account of self-defense."

"What would you do if you had the chance?"

Adan grew thoughtful, running his hand across his chin several times.

"I'd do what they did to my dad. I'd lock 'em up and throw the key away."

"Now you're talking."

47

JEREMY WAS UBERING AND ADAN WAS WORKING HIS shift at the restaurant while Noah and Zach talked in the living room. Noah considered Zach to be his equal. Unlike Jeremy, who could become volatile seemingly over nothing, Zach was steady and did not anger easily. He'd learned a lot in prison, especially how to exercise self control and stay out of trouble. At twenty-seven, he was the oldest of the roommates and the only one with a serious girlfriend.

"Grizz gave us twelve hundred for the bikes so that's three hundred apiece."

"Twelve hundred? That's nothing," Zach said, disappointed.

"That's what he gave us," Noah lied. He had a habit of shaving some of the profit off the top when he could. He thought of it as a fee for services rendered.

"Yeah, but they're worth so much more."

"Not to him. It was take it or leave it, so I took it. You win some, you lose some."

"Wait a minute," Zach said. "The kid had nothing to do

with that. It was just the three of us. We should be getting four hundred apiece."

"I was just thinking he could use the bucks and he did put us on to a big score."

"Not if we can't sell the stuff," Zach said, shaking his head. "We've never done anything like this. Shit, for all we know the radios are registered or they're so rare that as soon as you put it out there someone will know where it came from. Like the bikes."

Noah thought for a moment, switching through TV channels with the sound off.

"We can always say we bought it. Who's to say we didn't? We could say we paid cash. The whole thing depends on if they're reported stolen and I'll bet they won't be. The guy is dead and his relatives prolly just want his money."

Zach wasn't convinced, shaking his head.

"Forget it for now," Noah said. "We'll figure it out. If there's no police report on it we're free. But that's not what I wanna talk about."

Zach nodded.

"Why don't you settle on a ball game or something?" he said, annoyed by Noah's incessant channel surfing.

"I talked to Grizz about the kid, you know, being a fugitive and all."

"Yeah. What did he say?"

"He said to get rid of him."

Zach looked at Noah ambiguously.

"What does that mean?"

"Not sure, but don't tell Jeremy."

48

ALTHOUGH ADAN THOUGHT JEREMY TO BE A BIT creepy, he was the one who seemed most interested in him, willing to share time with him. Adan felt he might be able to trust him. He wanted to trust Noah and Zach as well but he saw less of them and felt he didn't know them as well. Besides, they were in their mid to late twenties, older than both himself and Jeremy. Even so, being seventeen meant that he was five years younger than his roommate, who had already spent time in prison and had a hard edge to him that Adan hadn't developed. He was also pushy. It was Jeremy who pushed Adan into getting tattoos. It was Jeremy who stepped in when Adan couldn't find his grandfather's gun. It was Jeremy who pressed him about race, a subject his grandfather harped on so much that Adan had learned to tune him out. Why be so upset about black people in a place where there weren't any? It was like worrying about sharks in Lake Michigan. The ostracism he'd faced as a white trash outsider was what he experienced, and though he didn't like it, he had learned to live with it. The bullying he'd experienced in high school occurred because he was an easy target with no one to defend him.

For his part, Jeremy was looking for allies to his cause. Zach was focused on his future and self-improvement and kept his nose clean. Noah was antiauthoritarian, which his body art made clear. He hated cops. He hated the rich. And he wasn't race friendly, as other tattoos made clear. Nonetheless, he could get along with anyone because it was better than getting in fights with everyone. But he wouldn't cross the street to punch a black man. Jeremy would not only cross the street, he'd chase him down an alley if he thought he could win, which was not often the case since what he gained in terms of rage he lacked in terms of physical force to back it up. But it didn't stop him from trying, annoying minorities by giving them the finger or shouting at them when they were on the sidewalk and he was in his car.

In addition to spending time with Adan, Jeremy would spring for lunch on drives around town when he would point out the various neighborhoods and places to avoid.

"You don't want to go there," he'd say, not actually entering the neighborhood as they drove by. "Don't want to be anywhere around here at night, 'less you're armed for bear, black bear."

Jeremy nodded and watched as they drove past what looked to him like normal neighborhoods compared to where he'd grown up. If anything, Jeremy's ceaseless chatter put Adan into a reverie, much like he'd felt on the bus ride into New Orleans, his head against the window, tired and dreamy, nothing on his mind until they'd hit a bump that shook him out of it or they'd stop in traffic when fear of discovery threatened to overwhelm him, as if they were stopping so that lawmen could take him to jail.

"Everybody's a racialist deep down," Jeremy said

quietly as they sat at a booth at a Burger King eating Whoppers. "It's like blood. Nothing runs deeper."

Adan looked down the counter where orders were taken.

"So, how come you let a black lady take your order?"

"That's different. I don't mind them working minimum wage jobs, and if you notice the cooks wear hairnets and gloves so they're never actually touching the food. But I know what you're saying. I wish everything was white, too."

"That's not what I'm saying," Adan responded. "I don't care who serves me food."

"Yeah, but how would you like to have to work for them?"

"Well, considering I've never had a real job—"

"They're just as big a racist as we are, don't kid yourself. Black power, the prison gangs, Black Lives Matter, they're all racist against whites, your own kind."

"Can we talk about something else?"

"Like what?"

"Like selling the radios."

"Oh, yeah. You scored big on that," Jeremy said, grinning, holding his fist up,

"Me?" Adan said, giving Jeremy a light bump.

"Well, it was your idea. Noah was impressed and he ain't easily impressed."

"Yeah, but we don't get paid until we sell them, right?"

Jeremy nodded while biting into his burger.

"How long does that take?"

Swallowing and washing it down with a Coke, Jeremy shrugged.

"Noah will figure it out. He's good at that. Prolly already has a plan. I know he was taking those bikes over to a guy so we should see some money soon."

Adan smiled.

"That'd be great. I'm running out of cash and the dish-washing job ain't cutting it. The hours suck and sometimes they don't need me so it's not like I'm getting enough hours."

"I hear that."

49

Noah's meeting with Grizz wasn't only about selling bikes and seeking advice about the fugitive in their midst. None of his roommates had met Chester Griswold, which was the way the old man wanted it. He trusted no one, not even Noah. It hadn't always been like that. Early on, his crew consisted of men his own age. They had similar experiences, grew up in the same milieu sharing the same cultural references. But they didn't last. Some died, some moved away, some were serving, some got out of the life. Those taking their places were younger, grew up in different eras, had different ideas from Griswold's hard knocks, old school traditions. They laughed behind his back at what he didn't know about technology. None of them had done hard time and as the age difference increased, he got to the point that they shared nothing in common. His doctor had told him that his infirmities were only going to get worse even though he'd stopped taking hormones and only worked out now to keep the muscle from turning into flab. But it was getting harder to do, more painful, and while he wasn't looking for a way out, he realized that sometime in the near future he would have no choice. He wanted to ease himself out, but he knew that time was not on his side. He told himself it was only coincidental that the plan he'd come up with was not only his boldest, potentially most rewarding heist but could even be his last, whether he got away with it or not.

The kids around him were all into electronics and video games. They were loud, obnoxious and impudent like their music and lived in a different world than he did. Their slang, their clothing, their haircuts made them stand out like peacocks. Things had been changing for a long time. It had been almost a year since he'd jacked a truck. Hijacking was something he'd been good at, but with the advent of GPS tracking and closed circuit television the risks had increased to the point that he had to find other, more vulnerable targets.

"What he told me," Noah had explained to Zach, "was that he's setting up an op, a big one."

"He gonna rob a casino? 'Cause if he is I don't want any part—"

"No, nothing like that. There's gonna be some kind of coin and gold show at some hotel or some place like that in a coupla weeks and he wants to let us in on it."

"No shit."

"He says it could be worth millions."

Zach shook his head slightly.

"What?" Noah said insistently.

"You can't sell rare coins. Everybody knows if they're stolen."

"Grizz says there's lotsa gold and diamonds and shit. I asked him about the coins and he said there's people who buy them and don't care where they come from. He says he knows someone can sell them."

"Yeah, for what? This sounds like the bikes."

"He didn't say how much we'd get but that's not the main thing anyway. It's the gold and shit. It don't take nothing to sell gold. But he didn't get into details. He wants to know if we're in first."

"Why don't he use his own crew?"

"He didn't say. I didn't push him on it. I was there to talk about Adan. This is just a bonus. We can take it or leave it."

50

IN THE DAYS FOLLOWING THE HEIST, ADAN AND JEREMY presented Noah with what they'd learned about the market for vintage radios. They'd searched exhaustively on the former owner's name only to find few references. Apparently, most of the radios he owned had been acquired in the distant past, before the popularization of the internet. They found no indication that he'd ever offered one for sale, much less purchased any on eBay or other sites.

"That's good to hear," Noah said as they discussed their findings. "It sounds like nobody but his family even knew what he was doing. That should make it a lot easier on us."

Adan outlined the sites he'd found that focused on vintage electronics, radios in particular.

"They've got price guides and everything," he said eagerly, "but I need to get the info off the tags to—"

"Well, what are you waiting for?" Noah asked.

Jeremy glanced at Adan and they were out the door on the way to the storage unit to inventory the collection. Jeremy was drawn to Adan's Sig Sauer, leaving Adan to transcribe the information on the tags into an iPad. Jeremy grew impatient, having inserted the pistol into his waist-band and trying various poses.

"What's taking so long?" he whined.

"It'd go faster if you helped," Adan said, peevishly.

Jeremy approached Adan, his right hand on the gun butt as if preparing to pull it out from under his belt.

"You talkin' to me, punk? You talkin' to me?" he said, drawing the pistol out, trying to channel Robert De Niro's character in *Taxi Driver* but doing it poorly.

"C'mon, get serious," Adan said. "You read the tags and I'll type."

Jeremy pointed the gun at Adan.

"You talkin' to me, punk?" Jeremy said, before slipping the gun into his pants pocket.

Asking Jeremy to help was a waste of time. Either he spoke too fast, only to break his words into painfully slow syllables, or he spoke too softly, only to raise his voice to a shout.

"What's wrong with you?" Adan said, exasperated.

"This is boring. I hate boring stuff. I'm a man of action."

"OK, fine, I'll do it myself."

Jeremy smiled, as if he'd won an argument, turning his attention to a closer examination of the hundreds of items lining the shelves. Holding up a sealed box of thumb drives, he said, "What do you s'pose we could get for this?"

"I don't know. Doesn't Noah set the price?"

"Screw Noah," Jeremy said bitterly.

Surprised by Jeremy's sudden hostility, Adan said nothing.

"Zach told me we're getting only twelve hundred bucks for the bikes."

"So?"

"They're worth fifteen thou. We're getting less than ten

cents on the dollar. That ain't right. I think when it comes to Griswold, Noah's a pussy."

"What do you mean?"

"Noah doesn't stand up to him. Instead he just goes along, you know, happy to get what he offers."

"How do you know? Maybe that's the best—"

"Bullshit," Jeremy said heatedly. "All we know about Grizz is what Noah tells us. He talks about him like he's the worst dude on the planet when what he is is a fucking middle man."

"Yeah, I don't know nothing about that."

"Of course you don't. Zach told me we're gettin' a measly four hundred bucks apiece for the bikes. None for you, by the way."

Not wanting to be drawn into an argument, Adan shrugged.

"It's better than nothing, I guess."

"Bullshit," Jeremy squawked as he approached Adan. "Look at all this shit around us. Look at it. Some of it's been in here for months. Months. And we're not making a dime off it. We take the risk and then we do nothing with it. I'm sick and tired of it. We should be making real dough and instead all our money is sitting on these shelves. Just look at all these radios. How long you think they're gonna sit here?"

"I don't know. Noah's the boss, right?"

"He ain't my boss, that's for sure," Jeremy said, his voice rising in pitch. "It'd serve him right if I took what's coming to me, took my share."

"All I know is I'm not entitled to any of it, other than the radios."

"Right," Jeremy sniffed. "And you think you're gonna get a fair share? You are so gullible. He'll figure out a way to Jew you out of your fair share. You wait and see."

"Why don't you talk to him about it?"

"Like that would do any good," Jeremy argued. "He'd throw me outta the house just like that and then where would I be? I don't want that. Not now. But if I had my share of stuff I'd be able to sell it for enough to start my own crew. That's what I'd do."

Adan refocused on his work as Jeremy broke off the conversation and started fiddling with one of the radios, working its dials, reading the tag and shaking his head.

"Look at this. This radio is worth fifteen hundred bucks. Fifteen hundred bucks. If we got that we'd get as much as we're getting for the bikes, and this was a thousand times easier to get and a lot easier to carry and we don't need no fucking middle man to sell 'em."

Jeremy examined another tag and sighed.

"I got an idea," he said calmly.

Adan didn't respond.

"You wanna hear it?"

Not really, Adan thought, but said nothing.

"You know, we could sell some of this stuff on the side. Noah doesn't come here that much, he mostly sends me like I'm the delivery boy. Fuck, that pisses me off, too. You never see Zach running errands for Noah like me."

"Zach doesn't own a car."

"He could use the van. No, Noah's got it in for me. It's so obvious. Look at how he told Zach about the bikes but I didn't know nothing until Zach told me. What's that about? I think he's getting ready to fuck me over."

Finished with his inventory, Adan realized Jeremy was having a conversation with himself. Blowing off steam, he thought. Nothing more. Sooner or later he would tire of it and snap out of his funk. They just needed to get out of the storage unit. Something about it set him off. Jeremy had never talked like that before. At least not to him.

"Well, I'm done. Let's go."

"You go, I need to check something."

Adan felt relief as he emerged into the sunlight, cradling the iPad. Zach had lent it to him and he couldn't wait to get back and transfer the data into a spreadsheet on his laptop. Then he'd update the values with current pricing. He was confident that most of the radios would be worth more than the amount on the tags. Standing next to Jeremy's Prius, he wondered what was taking his roommate so long. Adan couldn't help notice a bulge in one of Jeremy's pants pockets as he approached the car.

"What you got?" Adan asked.

"What do you mean?"

"In your pocket."

"My keys."

51

NOAH WONDERED WHOM HE COULD TRUST. ZACH WAS the only roommate who hadn't lied to him, he thought, though he could not be certain of it. Adan had lied about everything and Jeremy was no better, having lied about his status as a probation violator. But Zach was the guy he talked to if for no other reason than that he and Zach tended to be around the house at the same time. Jeremy was here and there on his Uber assignments and Adan liked to sleep late.

Noah and Zach were in the back yard. Noah sat on the weight bench while Zach sat in a lawn chair sipping coffee. The sun was out, the air was warm and humid, and Noah normally would be pumping iron but instead stared at a printout that Adan had given him the previous day. Adan had left it on Noah's bed but it fell on the floor and Noah hadn't seen it until he woke. It was an inventory of the radios. It listed everything from the tags, including the price, alongside which Adan had included current pricing. The total at the bottom of the page stunned Noah.

"This is what the kid gave me," Noah said, handing the spreadsheet to Zach.

Zach glanced at it and took another sip.

"Look at the total."

Zach shook his head in disbelief.

"Is that right?"

"I don't know, but according to him we've gone from a twenty thousand dollar haul to thirty six thousand bucks."

"Jesus," Zach said, returning the printout to Noah. "You think we can get that much?"

"I doubt it. But, still, I would never have guessed it. But it's not the only thing we got going on."

"Oh, really? What else you got?"

"Grizz wants us to help with that op he's setting up. I told you about it the other day."

"I remember," Zach said absently. "You didn't say much about it."

"He called me yesterday, which is unusual in itself. Asked if we're interested, again. He wouldn't do that if he didn't need us."

"Some sort of coin show, right?"

"Something like that. Gems, jewelry, gold. I asked but he won't say much more unless we're in. It's the biggest thing he's ever done, so, you know, it must be big. Real big."

"I don't know, man," Zach said, skeptically.

"What?"

"I don't mind the kinda shit we do, but this sounds like it's out of our league. I mean, he's just gonna go in there and they're just gonna hand everything over? I doubt it."

Noah frowned.

"He didn't explain everything. He just wants to know if we're in or not. I thought I'd ask you first."

Zach shook his head.

"Why does he want us?"

"I think because he's pissed off at some of the people he's been working with. He calls them punks."

"So, what do we get out of it?"

"A percentage of the take."

"And how much is that?"

Noah looked around him to make sure no one was listening. Then he leaned toward Zach, who leaned in.

"Half a million. Or more."

"What?"

"You heard me."

"That's our take?"

Noah nodded sagaciously.

"Oh, man," Zach said. "Jesus."

"Yeah. That's over a hundred thou each. But he says we'd hafta go live with him for awhile."

"Why?"

"Says we'll need to practice for it. We can't just bust in there. He's got a plan."

"What does he get out of it?"

"Knowing Grizz, he'll get plenty. What the fuck, man? You know anyone else with a better deal?"

52

Ever since his release from prison, Chester Griswold wanted nothing more than to make a lot of money quickly and never work another day in his life. That didn't happen. Years had passed during which he ran one job after another, old school smash and grabs, hijackings, mostly thefts, some of which turned into robberies. Nothing like what he was now planning. But he was in a quandary.

The only people he could trust were his old sidekicks, Horace Bone and Ray Gasser. The young guys were impetuous and disrespectful and he hated them and he didn't trust them. He worried about being caught, while the young guys didn't think such a thing was possible. They thought serving a few months in the parish lockup was like going to school. None of them had done real time. But he needed them, which is why he put some of them up in his compound when they matriculated out of jail. They understood the internet and cyber crime. They needed a place to stay. They set up and managed his wi-fi network. They showed him how to use The Onion Router. They ran ops using a credit card skimmer, which floored him. He'd seen them do it just sitting outdoors at a coffee shop, stealing credit card data from passersby. The success rate wasn't high, but all they needed was one or two and then they encoded a blank credit card and it was off to the mall. This was the kind of thing he wished he'd gotten into years ago, but now catching up was almost impossible.

The young guys were cocky and always thought they knew better than the old guys. And maybe they did. He was no different than before prison. They were making a good living fencing things for him on the internet that he couldn't do on his own. He had his contacts in Mexico and points south but that was mostly for conspicuous items, cars in particular, of which there were fewer and fewer. Other gangs had horned in on the car action, drying up what was once a lucrative business. And other than showing him how they did it, the youngsters didn't share their proceeds with him, not that he had expected them to share given he had nothing to do with their ops.

Griswold had known Noah for more than two years and he made decent money fencing Noah's stuff, but it didn't generate the kind of profits that he wanted. The bicycles were the largest item he'd fenced for him in months.

Perhaps the worst thing for Griswold was that he didn't really know the young guys, who came and went like migratory birds. His place at one time was something of a revolving door for young criminals. Mostly, they came after release and some of them were gone within weeks. Only the losers, mostly the ones who lacked cyber skills, remained for a month, but eventually even they figured out how to make it without Griswold's help. They paid rent, bought their own food and contributed labor on the many remodeling and repair projects around the compound but it wasn't like his old crews, where everyone was part of something larger.

He hadn't told them about his coin and gem op. In fact, Noah was the only person who knew about it, and he didn't know much. He felt Noah was a good judge of character and that he'd never let anyone live with him whom he couldn't trust, so he was hoping that Noah's entire crew would come along and provide the manpower the old man would need to pull it off. He figured it would take no more than seven men, including himself, to do a takeover, grab the most profitable stuff and be gone within minutes. There would be security, obviously.

But he had a plan for that in the locked room where he kept his firearms and ammunition.

53

BEFORE GOING TO WORK, NOAH EXPLAINED GRISWOLD'S proposal to his crew. Zach, who already knew about it, watched how Jeremy and Adan reacted. He was still weighing the op in his own mind, figuring out the pros and cons. His girlfriend didn't know about his thievery, only that he'd spent time in jail and that he was turning his life around. They'd been discussing whether he should move in with her. Ambitious, she had dreams of starting a business and thought Zach would be a good business and romantic partner. Zach had attended a franchise convention with her and liked the idea of working for himself as a law-abiding citizen.

Jeremy liked the idea of a one hundred thousand dollar payday so much that he didn't sign in to Uber until after noon. With Zach and Noah having gone to work, Jeremy was like a kid with a secret too big to keep. His mind was flooded with images of all the things he could do with that kind of money, starting with women. He could trade in his Prius on a babe magnet.

"I'd get a Mustang GT convertible or a Challenger with

a 392," he told Adan while fantasizing about what they would do with the money. "What're you gonna do with yours?"

Adan shrugged.

"I'm not gonna do anything. Can't afford to."

"Whadya mean? You'll have a hundred K."

"The cops are looking for me. I can't afford to stick out."

"So, you're just gonna sit in your room all day?"

"No, nothin' like that," Adan objected. "I'll do something, just don't know what. Get a better ID, that's one thing. I've been readin' up on it and you can get passports that fool the feds. Same with driver's licenses. That's what the rich illegals do when they come here. But you gotta know someone and you gotta pay a lot. So, that's what I'd do right off the bat."

"Doesn't sound like as much fun as a GT, but you ain't me."

"But you're on parole, right?"

"Probation. I'm on probation," Jeremy protested. "But I'm not worried about it. If I get caught, I get caught. Meanwhile, I'm gonna have a good time."

"So, you don't worry about it?"

"Not really. Even if they catch me, it's not like I'm running from an attempted murder charge like you. I'll just serve my time, be a model prisoner, and when I get released I'll still have all that money. It's a freaking dream come true."

Adan smiled faintly. Depressed by his situation, he didn't like to think about it, so he changed the subject.

"Think it'll work?"

Still imagining himself in a fancy car surrounded by hot babes, Jeremy ignored the question.

"Have you ever done anything like it?"

Putting his fantasy aside for the moment, Jeremy shook his head.

"Nope. 'Course, Noah didn't say much. Prolly doesn't know much."

"But you're OK with it?" Adan asked, tentatively. "I mean, he said we'd have to move and get trained. What kind of training?"

"Don't know. Don't care. But it's kinda amazing when you think about it?"

"What's amazing?"

"Well, for starters, you find this hoard of radios that are worth a fortune and now we get a shot at the big time. It's like winning the lottery twice."

Jeremy was all in on the fantasy while Adan struggled with the reality of his vulnerability. Of the four, he had the most to risk, and now that they were planning on something big he started to wonder whether it was time to move on. He had felt no fear in stealing the radios and, after the research he'd done, he was confident they would all make good money and that they could sell the radios with very little risk. Even selling them at half their value, they'd each pocket an easy five thousand apiece.

"So, what do you think?" Jeremy asked. "This is something that can change your life, man. For the better. I'll be outta this place like a bullet when it's over. You too, man. You get that new ID and you'll be gold. You'll be able to start over anywhere you want."

"Not Texas," Adan said, glumly. "I can't ever go back there."

"Well, that leaves the rest of the world, don't it? Take it from me, bro, you don't get many chances like this."

54

ADAN SPENT THE AFTERNOON ALONE, ANTSY AS HELL. He lifted weights to try to burn off the anxiety but couldn't keep focused. If only he could concentrate on selling the radios, earn the trust of his roommates, become a full participant in the crew. He'd be satisfied with that. He had no burning desire to leave, not when by fits and starts he had grown comfortable with his situation. It didn't bother him that he couldn't get a driver's license. It was just one of the things he had to give up to protect himself. But walking around with an ID that his roommates dissed as soon as they saw it bothered him. It was good enough to fool the people at the restaurant and the homeless shelter, but it wasn't as if they were looking for a reason to kick people out. Maybe they knew and didn't care. Maybe they were just accustomed to people lying to them.

Unlike Jeremy, who fixated on the reward and not the risk, Adan couldn't simply dismiss it. It was always there in the back of his mind. Seeing a police car made him uneasy. Seeing cops on horseback made him change direction. Seeing them on the sidewalk gave him goosebumps. That's why he wore sunglasses, to protect himself. If they couldn't see his eyes, they couldn't see the guilt that he carried around like a knapsack. Maybe if he was drunk or high, he could escape it, but having watched his alcoholic grandfather for half his life he knew he didn't want to end up like him. He wondered if anti-anxiety meds would help. That was another thing he'd researched. He knew the names of the drugs, and read about how people were affected by them, but he worried whether they would change his personality, making him less cautious, more likely to make a mistake that would land him in prison. It was a terrible situation. Every time he thought of something that might help, he found reasons that either it wouldn't or would make things worse. One of these days he'd ask Jeremy. He knew that his roommate used drugs that Noah didn't want in the house. What Jeremy called "happy pills."

Maybe they'd let him work the radios while they pulled off the big op. That's what he hoped, but he couldn't just come out and say it for fear they'd think less of him. He had to pull his own weight and that meant doing things he didn't want to do, taking risks he didn't want to take.

55

Given that Jeremy thought Adan would be a wuss if he declined to join the crew for the big op and given that at seventeen Adan couldn't see a future beyond being part of Noah's crew, the teenager nodded in the affirmative when Jeremy asked him point blank whether he was in or out.

"I'm in," Adan said, but not with enough enthusiasm to satisfy his roommate.

"Say it like you mean it, bro," Jeremy insisted.

"I'm in," Adan said, loudly for him. "I'm in, OK?"

Not wanting to push it, Jeremy, whose enthusiasm for the job was limited only by his fantasies, smiled. This was the big score he'd always wanted. The winning ticket. A chance to throw off the shackles that bound him to Noah's stifling house rules and branch out on his own. No women overnight. No social media. *The cops can read everything you type*, Noah claimed. Even so, he was pumped. He felt like an up and coming rock star. At the same time, he'd noticed that Noah and Zach weren't as excited as he was.

Noah had told them to think about it for a day, as if there was some reason not to do it.

"It's the biggest thing we've ever done, by far," Noah had told them. "And we don't know how it's gonna go down and we won't know unless we're all in."

Jeremy figured Noah knew more than he was telling but the important part was how much loot they'd earn. He had no reason to doubt him on that score. Noah's caution may have kept them out of trouble, though it frustrated Jeremy who sometimes couldn't be himself, couldn't be as free with his money as he wanted. When they gathered for the vote, Noah explained that it had to be unanimous.

"Why's that?" Jeremy said sharply. "Every other vote we've had it was majority rule."

"It's too big for that," Noah said.

"My problem is that we don't know much about it," Zach said soberly.

"That's all I know," Noah said. "I've got questions, too, but Grizz isn't gonna give us anymore info unless we're on board. Shit, he already took a chance telling me."

"He needs us or he wouldn't have asked," Zach said.

Jeremy nudged Adan, who was sitting next to him on the couch.

"Maybe he can't do it without us," Jeremy said. "Maybe we should be asking for a better deal."

"You want to go over there and negotiate?" Noah asked sarcastically.

Jeremy knew better than to get into an argument when what he wanted was to make a decision.

"Why don't we vote on it and get it over with?"

Noah saw that both Jeremy and Adan were ready to raise their hands while Zach was looking at the floor, his hands clasped between his legs.

"I'm moving in with my lady," Zach said quietly.

"What?" Noah said, surprised.

"We been thinking about it for awhile and she's ready and, I don't know, I'm ready for a different life."

"How can you say that?" Jeremy seethed. "Goddamn it. You can't just walk away from this."

"I can if I want to," Zach said defiantly. "It's my life. I never made it a secret that I want to stop living like this. Y'all know that. Well, maybe not you, Adan, but the rest of you do."

"I thought that was like down the line," Noah said.

"Yeah, what about the rest of us?" Jeremy said. "You can't just walk out on us like this."

"I'm not walking out on anybody. I'm just moving to Jessie's apartment."

"Bull. Shit," Jeremy said angrily, rising.

"Calm down," Noah said. "And sit down. We're all friends here. We just have to work this out."

Shaking his head, Jeremy's expression changed from expectation to outrage.

"I will not sit down for this," he fumed. "I'm counting on this and I'm in whether y'all are or not. Me and Adan," he said, glancing at the teen. "Right?"

Adan nodded meekly.

"What about you, Noah? What's your vote?"

"When are you moving out?" Noah asked Zach.

"Next week, I was thinking."

"So you're out of the op, right?" Jeremy demanded.

"I told you to sit down," Noah said, harshly. "You know the rules. We don't get in each other's face. Now sit down."

Jeremy took a deep breath, looked at Adan and returned to his seat, still seething.

"This is not how I thought things would work out," Noah said.

"If Zach is out, can't the three of us do it anyway?" Jeremy asked, still bristling with anger.

"Grizz said he needed the four of us. That's all I know."

"Look," Zach said. "Let me talk to Jessie."

"You're gonna tell her about this?"

"Of course not. But I gotta explain why I won't be around for a coupla weeks. It's gonna take that long, right?"

Noah nodded. Zach said he'd talk to his girlfriend after work.

"And after that, it's over for me," he said sharply, staring at Jeremy.

"Works for me," Jeremy said acerbically.

56

Noah had no way of knowing what Griswold's plan was beyond what he had told his crew, but having worked with him for the past two years he trusted him almost as much as he had trusted Zach before the unexpected announcement that he was leaving. He knew Zach would leave one day but Noah was surprised at the timing. He wondered now whether he could depend on Zach, knowing that his future lay elsewhere. Jeremy got under his skin and pissed him off so much that he had been thinking of throwing him out. But he also feared him, not physically but his tendency to go ballistic. He worried about him doing something stupid and getting jailed and maybe using what he knew about Noah's operation to bargain for a lighter sentence. It happened all the time. It was one of the risks he took, but that's why he set rules and expected everyone to abide by them, whether they liked them or not. It would have been so much easier if he were the violent sort who could put the fear of God into those around him. Like Griswold. But he wasn't, which made dealing with people like Jeremy problematic.

Because of the way his crew was unraveling, Noah felt he had no choice but to talk to Griswold about it. He was the only other person he could trust. There was no doubt people were afraid of him. He was big, had a reputation for violence and there were rumors that he'd sent more than one person to his grave. But he'd always been cordial in their dealings. Now that he needed his crew he might be willing to help Noah solve his own problems.

"I don't like going into this knowing nothing," Noah said as he met with Griswold at a dive bar in Metairie.

"Your guys are in?"

"Yeah, but, you know, they want to know more."

"Tough shit," Griswold said. "This is one of those once-in-a-lifetime deals and if that ain't good enough for 'em tell them to go fuck themselves."

"C'mon, Grizz, don't be that way."

"I can find another crew if I need to," Griswold insisted. "It's just that I know you pretty well and I like the way you operate. You're disciplined, which is more than I can say for ninety percent of the assholes who come my way. I wouldn't have told you about it if I didn't trust you. But I don't know your guys."

"Well, three of us are ready and the fourth one has to deal with his girlfriend."

"Why don't he just dump the bitch?"

"She doesn't know what he does for a living. He just has to come up with an excuse why he won't be around for a coupla weeks."

"Pussy whipped."

"He'll figure it out."

"What about the rest? Any other problems?"

"I might have to quit my job, but that's not a big deal. So would the other guys. Can you give us till next week?"

"I'll give you until tomorrow. We need to move on this."

57

THE LIVING ARRANGEMENT IN GRISWOLD'S COMPOUND was much the same as it had been at the house. Zach and Noah shared a room, as did Jeremy and Adan. The rooms were larger and each had its own bathroom and entry onto a common walkway that opened onto what had once been an asphalt parking lot but was evolving into a junkyard. Piles of scrap lumber and metal rose from the asphalt like asymmetrical pyramids. Cars, including Noah's van and Jeremy's car, were parked near the entry gate. The entire complex was surrounded by tall sheet metal fencing topped with razor wire. Griswold occupied one wing of the L-shaped, two-story concrete block building that he'd remodeled, while the remainder was left much as it had been when it operated as a low-rent motel. Other rooms were occupied by two guys about Griswold's age, one of whom worked the gate to let Noah's crew inside.

"Look at that old fart," Jeremy told Adan as they drove into the compound. The man wore denim coveralls over a checked short-sleeve shirt topped with a Saints cap and a graying pony tail. "He looks like a fucking farmer."

The four met outside Noah's room before proceeding to Griswold's side of the building. None were impressed with the condition of the building or the parking lot, which was scarred by lumps of buckling asphalt.

"I thought I was gonna tear out my transmission," Jeremy said.

"You've been here before, right?" Zach asked Noah.

"Yeah. It was worse the first time I came out. He's fixing it up."

"Doesn't look like he's in a hurry," Jeremy said.

"His place is pretty nice," Noah said. "He's done a lot of work there. Knocked out walls and shit. That's where the kitchen is."

"I was gonna ask what we do for food."

"And drink," Jeremy said. "I could use a beer."

"I take it the guy at the gate wasn't Grizz," Zach said.

"There's a couple of old guys hang around here," Noah said. "Sometimes there's young guys but I haven't seen any in a while."

"No surprise there," Jeremy said. "Who'd want to stay here?"

"Oh, somebody fresh outta jail," Noah said, "like me. I stayed here when I got out. That's how I got to rent the house from Grizz, once I got settled."

"Is he like a slumlord all over town?"

Noah shot Jeremy a withering look.

"Do you gotta criticize everything, for chrissakes? As I recall, you were really happy when I took you in to my slum."

Jeremy smiled crookedly.

"Sorry, boss," he said, running a finger across his lips.

58

CHESTER GRISWOLD WAS WATCHING A FOOTBALL GAME on the seventy five-inch plasma in his man cave when Horace Bone let him know that Noah's crew had arrived. Like Griswold, Bone was heavily tatted. Unlike Griswold, Bone had let his once muscular body devolve into a mountain of flab, making a mockery of his tats, which he mostly hid under his shirt and coveralls.

"How they look?"

"Like kids," Bone said.

"Well, we need 'em so—"

"I got it. I'm not gonna fuck with 'em. I'll get Ray."

"Do that. We need to meet with these guys."

"You're sure about them, right?"

"No, but what choice do we have?"

"Got it."

Bone, large enough to fill the doorway, crossed paths with Noah's crew as they opened the door to enter Griswold's domain. They stepped aside to let him pass.

"Man," Jeremy whispered, "he needs a bath. Whew."

"Knock it off," Noah scolded. "Remember why we're here."

"I remember," Jeremy said. "To get rich. I'll do whatever it takes."

"I hope that includes shutting up," Zach said, irritated.

Once again, Jeremy ran his finger across his lips

Griswold's home looked nothing like the rest of the compound. The light grey tile floor was shared by an open concept kitchen, dining and living areas, leading into a hallway that ran to the back of the building. Track lighting in the living and dining areas created islands of light over the six-foot long oak dining table and a conversation pit consisting of a pair of facing dark red leather matching club chairs and facing sofas. Recessed lighting brightened the kitchen, which was equipped with high-end stainless appliances.

The young men marveled at the interior.

"This looks like one of those TV shows," Zach said.

Jeremy responded with a puzzled look.

"You know, where they buy houses, remodel them and flip them."

Jeremy glanced at Adan. Neither knew what show Zach was referring to.

"Yeah, he's put a lot of money and time into this," Noah said.

"He does all the work himself?" Zach asked.

"I don't know. Looks good, though."

Jeremy and Adan drifted to the conversation pit and tried out the club chairs.

"Boy, these are big," Adan said, as he sank into the seat cushion.

"You saw that guy with the pony tail," Jeremy quipped.

"Big chairs for big guys. But where's the TV? They gotta have a TV, right."

"There's one in our room."

"I tried it. It don't work. Anyway, it's a piece of crap, must be older than me."

Joined by Noah and Zach, who sat on one of the sofas, Jeremy repeated his question.

"He's got a TV room down the hall," Noah said. "That's probably where he is. He likes watching sports."

"Why don't he come out and see us?" Jeremy asked, impatiently tapping his foot. "We been here like five minutes already."

Noah wouldn't admit it but he agreed with Jeremy. This was a business deal and they shouldn't be kept waiting. At the same time, he was reluctant to barge in on the big man. But, at Jeremy's prompting, he got up anyway and headed toward the hallway when the front door opened. Horace Bone had returned with Ray Gasser, another old guy, only rail thin and tall. Griswald thought they looked like Laurel and Hardy. The two headed toward the hallway, ignoring Noah as they passed by.

"Ray's here, Grizz," Bone said into the doorway leading to the man cave. "He was just making sure the kids weren't followed."

GRISWOLD STEADIED HIMSELF BEFORE LEAVING HIS media room, lit by the glow of the plasma. Wearing a long purple robe secured at the waist, he painfully worked out the stiffness in his joints, his initial steps revealing a limp that dissipated as he made his way into the living room, followed by Bone and Gasser, to greet his guests. Noah and his crew watched as he approached, stopping in front of Jeremy. Griswold lifted his head slightly, as if sending a signal. Jeremy looked up, grinning slightly, tentatively offering his hand.

"You're in the boss's chair," Bone said, his gravelly voice the result of a lifetime of smoking.

"Sorry," Jeremy said, moving to a place on Noah's sofa.

After settling into the club chair, Griswold eyed the young men briefly.

"You want anything to drink?" he asked.

"What you got?" Jeremy asked.

Griswold glanced at Bone and Gasser.

"What you want?" Bone asked.

"How about a beer?"

Bone glanced at Griswold.

"We got water. You want water?"

Jeremy stopped smiling and leaned back, shaking his head.

"Anyone else?" Griswold asked, as he motioned for Bone and Gasser to sit on the second sofa. Air whooshed out of the cushions under Bone's three hundred pounds.

"Before I tell you anything, y'all tell me what you know about this gig."

The four young men looked at each other, as if determining who would respond. Jeremy eyed Noah.

"Shouldn't we like introduce ourselves first?" Jeremy asked.

Griswold glanced at his partners and shook his head.

"I told them what you told me," Noah said, giving Jeremy a cross look.

"So you know, this ain't like a B and E. This is big time. Might be the biggest thing you do your whole life."

"But when we're done, we'll be rich, right?" Jeremy interrupted. "That's what Noah told us."

Noah's head dropped. He eyed the coffee table and its spread of *Architectural Digest* and remodeling magazines.

Griswold exhaled slowly, his eyes narrowing as he sized up Jeremy.

"That's right. You'll be rich. But let me tell you, that might be the hardest thing of all."

Bone and Gasser smiled slightly, as if at an inside joke.

"Lotsa guys get caught because they do stupid things with the money, like buying expensive cars and shit. They blow it on drugs, women and casinos and end up worse than when they started."

"What good is it if you can't spend it?" Jeremy asked.

"Nobody said you couldn't spend it," Griswold said, his voice rising. "There's two parts to this—the doing of it and the getting away with it. I got no doubt we can do it. But I don't know about the rest. Me and the boys here will get away with it 'cause we know how not to draw attention to ourselves. I don't know about you guys. And let me make one thing clear as day, you fuck up and it brings attention to us, you won't have to worry about how to spend it. You can be damn sure I ain't going to the joint again on account of any fuck ups."

Noah and Zach looked at each other nervously.

"No whispering," Griswold scolded Noah. "You got something to say, say it."

"You're talking about if one of us does something stupid after the op, right?"

"Yeah, yeah, that's what I said," Griswold nodded, glancing at his partners for confirmation.

"That's what I heard," Bone said.

"I just want to make sure you understand how this works, how me and my boys work. You be straight with me and I'll be straight with you. Understood?"

Noah looked for affirmation from the others. No one objected.

"Tell you what. You talk it over and we'll get together in the morning. Meanwhile, leave your cell phones on the table."

"What? Why?" Noah demanded.

"My party, my rules," Griswold said.

56

"This is shit, man," Zach said as the four returned to their rooms. "We don't even know what we're gonna do and he threatens us."

"And he takes our phones," Jeremy complained. "What's with that? I'm naked without my phone."

"I don't think of it as a threat. You don't know him. That's the way he is. He talks tough," Noah said.

"He looks tough," Adan said. "Like my gramps."

"Why take the phones?" Zach asked.

"He doesn't want word to get out, I guess," Noah said unconvincingly.

"He don't scare me," Jeremy said defiantly. "If I wanna buy a car, I'll buy a car. I don't care what the old man says."

"He didn't say you can't buy a car," Noah said. "What he means is that because you have lots of money you gotta be careful."

"How do we know we can trust him?" Zach asked somberly.

"That's the fifty thousand dollar question," Jeremy said.

"How do we know if we can trust anybody?" Noah said. "You either do or you don't. I trust him. I've been dealing with him for more than two years and he's never gone back on his word or anything."

"Yeah, but that's for penny ante stuff compared to this," Zach said. "And we still don't know what he's planning except—"

"We know what it is, we just don't know how we're gonna do it," Noah said.

"Yeah, yeah, it's like a gun show only with gold and emeralds and shit," Jeremy said.

"I just wish we knew more about how he's gonna do it," Zach said.

Noah nodded in agreement but harbored doubts about Zach's commitment. Nothing like a girlfriend to screw things up. Even so, he trusted Zach more than the others. He was a rock compared to Jeremy. He liked Adan but

Adan remained a cypher to him if for no other reason than Noah didn't see him as much as the others. But he couldn't dismiss the fact that the seventeen-year-old was a fugitive and could bring down his entire operation should he be caught. How likely was it that he wouldn't implicate him and the others, if it came to that? But that was a problem with any criminal act involving more than one person. How far could he trust anyone?

"Let's just take another vote and get this over with. Are we in or not?"

57

"I already don't like that skinny shithead," Griswold said. "He reminds me of some of the assholes who stayed here. What is it with kids these days?"

"I know what you mean, Grizz," Bone said.

"He's gotta go, boss," Gasser said, lisping slightly. "He's a hot head."

Bone and Gasser didn't have much going for them. They were old, slow, and their skill set had long ago become obsolete. They'd been with Grizz since forever and knew what he was thinking just by looking at him. They were loyal as hell. Anything Grizz wanted to do, they'd do it. Bone had served time for bank robbery while Gasser got caught up on a jewelry heist on the East Coast. Neither of them was interested in returning to prison.

"We gotta keep 'em busy," Griswold continued. "Get 'em used to handling the guns."

"Think we can trust them that far?"

Griswold eyed his partners, his head nodding slightly as if from a tremor.

"Noah, maybe, not the rest of them."

"You know, they never done nothing like this," Gasser said.

"Neither have we," Bone said.

"Yeah, but—"

"Don't matter," Griswold said. "We got a plan and as long as we stick with it, we'll be fine."

"What about them?"

"What about 'em?"

"Will they stick with the plan? Especially after."

Gasser grinned.

58

The second vote turned out like the first. Jeremy was already counting his money, Noah convinced Zach that he'd have enough money to start a business with his girlfriend, though he continued to harbor doubts about the op. Adan had become accustomed to going along with whatever Jeremy wanted. Noah planned to cut ties with everyone, though he kept it to himself. Just like he didn't tell them that he'd quit his job.

"I thought you said you were gonna quit?" Griswold asked Noah when he told him how the vote came out.

"I thought about it. Seemed like a better idea to just stay on,"

"Not sure I like that," Griswold said.

"It's only during the afternoon. The other guys quit what they were doing."

"So why couldn't you just quit?"

"Got a bad vibe about quitting."

They were sitting at one end of Griswold's rectangular mahogany dining table, sipping coffee. When it looked as if Noah was going to set his cup on the table, Griswold handed him a coaster.

"Sounds like bullshit to me."

Noah exhaled a bubble of air between his closed lips.

Looking around to make sure they were alone, he drew closer to Griswold.

"Between me and you, I'm making some changes. I'm gonna ditch these guys when it's over. So you know, I gotta prepare. I'm putting my stuff in storage. I quit my job but I'm not telling the guys."

Griswold smirked.

"What would happen if I told them?"

"You can kiss your op goodbye, that's for sure."

"What are you sayin'?"

"Just that if they find out what I'm doin' they'll bail. I'll bet on it. But, you know, I gotta take care of myself."

"So, you got another place?"

"I'm thinking about moving to Alaska, or Montana or somewhere where there ain't a lot of people."

"Alaska, huh?"

"Yeah," Noah smiled.

"Ever been there?"

"Nope. Just read about it and seen those shows about trappers and people living out in the wilderness. I could do that, 'specially if I got a lotta money to start with. I figure most of the people on those shows are just getting by 'cause they didn't think about the costs. Some of them live in shacks and tents, for chrissakes. Even in the winter. Not me."

"Gets cold there and there's bears."

"I know that. I'll have a gun or two. Everyone's got guns in Alaska. And I'll have money so I won't, you know, have to live off the land. At least not to start with. Maybe eventually. Who knows? Anyway, it's something I want to do."

"Just so you know, that punk kid, what's his name, the skinny one?"

"Oh, Jeremy."

"Yeah. Jeremy. He keeps up like he is and things could happen."

Noah's expression turned serious.

"Just so you know. Won't be any warning. It'll just happen. I don't tolerate fuck ups."

59

Keeping Noah's crew busy was a major part of the ten days leading up to the op. Griswold drilled them incessantly on their roles during the robbery, working off a floor plan he'd downloaded from the venue's web site, stripped of identifiers. Clearly, it wasn't a hotel as he'd let Noah to believe. He timed them and had them do it over and over until they thought they could do it in their sleep. He gave them toy guns to hold. They wore identical masks, coveralls and billed hats during the drills. When they weren't drilling, they were put to work cleaning up the compound and painting. Jeremy complained to Noah about it.

"This is chickenshit," Jeremy argued, twirling his toy six shooter, as they walked toward Noah's van. "He doesn't let us drink. He makes us do grunt work like hired hands. He takes our phones. You're lucky you got a job to go to. At least you get outta here once in a while. What's it like on the outside, by the way?"

"I'm a dishwasher, for cryin' out loud," Noah said harshly. "What do you think it's like? You wanna go work my job?"

"Shit, no," Jeremy said. "That reminds me. How come Adan's not working?"

"He's got no car and I'm not letting him use the van. You wanna let him use your car?"

"No way, bro. But these toy guns. Man, is that what we're gonna use? What kinda op is this?"

"I don't know any more than you," Noah said as he

reached the van. "Maybe he's testing us. Maybe he thinks we ain't got what it takes."

Jeremy sniffed, pointing the toy pistol at the van, squeezing the trigger, firing several imaginary bullets into the windshield.

"I got what it takes."

60

ZACH DIDN'T LIKE THE IDEA OF ARMED ROBBERY BUT grudgingly accepted it when Noah insisted that the guns would be for show.

"No one's gonna shoot anybody," Noah said, after returning from work and sneaking in a twelve pack.

"You got a pizza to go with that?"

Noah put the beer into the mini-fridge.

"Don't tell Jeremy or Adan about this," Noah said. "It's just for us."

Zach smiled appreciatively.

"What'd you have for supper?" Noah asked.

"The fat guy made shrimp po'boys. They were good."

"Food's not bad here, is it?"

"I was thinking we'd be eating fried chicken all the time, not that I don't like fried chicken. I could eat it every day. I won't ask you what you had."

"I had porchetta and potato gnocchi," Noah said, smacking his lips. "Thanks for asking."

"Good thing I don't know what that is," Zach said. "So, when can we have a beer?"

"Later."

61

THE PIÈCE DE RÉSISTANCE OF GRISWOLD'S PLAN WAS hidden behind a locked steel door in the back of his man cave. Satisfied that the young men could follow orders, he brought them together one evening, had them sit at the dining table and handed a beer to each of them.

"Use the coasters," he admonished. "This is a seven thousand dollar table. Show some respect."

"I know I been workin' you hard," he started. "You done good enough to get to this stage where we talk about the hardware. You understand, we got armament but we don't want to use it unless we have to. And if it comes to that, we probably won't get a dime out of this. So, we don't want that."

Pausing, he studied their young faces. Bone and Gasser, who sat on stools at the white granite kitchen island, watched. Griswold gave them time to drink. He wanted them to relax.

"So, what kind of *armament* are you talking about?" Jeremy asked, using air quotes for emphasis.

One side of Griswold's face broke into a smile as if he'd

had some kind of tic, unnerving Jeremy, who lowered his head, staring at the table top.

"Did you see that?" Zach whispered.

"Yeah, I think," Noah whispered.

Nodding to Bone and Gasser, Griswold stood and led the way. Noah and his crew admired the flat screen, wondering whether it was LED or plasma.

"It's plasma," Griswold said in passing. "Better blacks than LED."

"Not hardly," Jeremy whispered to Adan.

Illuminated by track lighting on a dimmer switch, the room was dark, the light seemingly absorbed by the black ceiling and walls. Three large leather recliners were arranged in front of the screen.

"It's a 7.1 sound system," Griswold said as he moved toward a wall covered with dark curtains descending from the ceiling. "It's got an Anthem receiver."

"You should hear the bass," Bone said. "It's like thunder."

While the crew admired the electronics, Griswold pushed the curtain aside near the center of the wall, revealing the steel door. Unlocking it with a key, he pulled it open and lights flickered inside, as if awakening to a new day. Within seconds, the ten-by-ten-foot room was filled with light, revealing a trove of weaponry arrayed on the walls.

"Wow. This is more like it," Jeremy said as he entered, stepping around a pedestal covered with a blanket in the room's approximate center.

With Bone and Gasser waiting in the man cave, the four young men circled the room admiringly.

"What are all these?" Zach asked.

"You name it, we got it," Griswold said, proudly. "ARs,

sawed-offs, a fifty cal sniper gun, even an M60. Some real bad boys here."

"What's an M60?" Noah asked.

"Machine gun," Jeremy said. "Real serious stuff."

"We got handguns, too."

"Ever use this?"

"Just for target practice," Griswold replied. "We got a place in the country where we shoot 'em off. We'll take you guys out there tomorrow. Let you get a feel for the hardware, get in some practice. Any of you have much experience with guns?"

Adan raised his hand.

"Ever shoot anything like an AR?"

"No, sir. Just pistols and a rifle."

"You're the one who shot that kid in Texas, right?"

"Yes, sir," Adan said, sheepishly.

"From what Noah told me, you were defending yourself. Nothing wrong with that," Griswold said as he ushered the men out of the gun room, locking the door behind them. Emerging into the hallway, Griswold explained his plan for the next day, most of which would be devoted to target practice.

"So, these are the guns we'll actually carry, not the toys we've been using. Is that right?" Jeremy asked.

"That's right," Griswold said.

"What was that thing on the pedestal?" Noah asked.

"You'll see in a day or two. Any other questions?"

"Can we have another beer?" Jeremy asked.

62

Horace Bone stood near Noah's van as he and his crew prepared to follow Griswold's Ford Expedition to a place in the boondocks for target practice.

Moments later, the Ford pulled alongside the van. As Bone hoisted himself into the big SUV, Griswold told Noah to follow him, but not too closely.

"Just don't let me get outta sight. You might get lost or miss the place. One other thing, no speeding. Signal your turns. Got it?"

"What the fuck was that all about?" Jeremy asked as they got underway.

"He's paranoid," Zach said.

"Or he don't trust us," Noah said.

"What the fuck am I gonna do without my phone?" Jeremy complained. "I hope it's not a long drive."

"You can do what you usually do," Zach said. "You can bitch."

"Fuck you."

"Enough," Noah said. "We gotta get along for another week. Let's just stay focused until it's over."

An hour into the drive, past Hammond on U.S. 55, the Ford turned off the highway and followed a maze of narrowing state and parish roads twisting through forests thick with loblolly pine and cypress. Zach nodded off in the shotgun seat while Adan stared out the window at the passing scenery and snowy white egrets. Even Jeremy was quiet, road noise making it difficult to conduct a conversation. Then they slowed as the Ford turned onto a single lane, tree-lined dirt road marked with a pair of prominent Posted signs. The road ended a half mile later in a small, weedy clearing where they parked.

"Where are we?" Adan asked sleepily as he and the others piled out of the van.

"No idea," Noah said.

"We're in the middle of nowhere," Jeremy said, stretching and yawning. "I don't see a shooting range, do you?"

"Hey, guys," Griswold shouted as he opened the Ford's hatch. "Time's a wastin'."

"All right," Jeremy said enthusiastically, rushing toward Griswold. "This is what I been waiting for."

63

"That was sick," Jeremy said cheerfully, sipping a beer in Noah and Zach's room. They were all so excited after a day spent shooting fully automatic weapons that all they could do was talk about it through the night.

"You been holding out on us," Jeremy said when Noah handed him a beer from his previously secret stash. "How long you had this?"

"Bought it yesterday. Haven't had any 'til now. You gonna complain, then gimme the beer back," Noah said, holding his hand out.

"I'm not complaining," Jeremy said, smiling. "You gotta admit those ARs are awesome. Man, one of them and you're like king of the world."

"Yeah, they're nice," Noah agreed.

"I just wish they'd brought the M60. That would have been awesome," Jeremy said.

"They ain't gonna let any of us use it," Noah said. "But like Grizz said, the whole point is to not use the guns."

"I kinda hope we do," Jeremy said, "you know, shoot

into the ceiling like they do in the movies. You know, to get people's attention."

"And what if the bullets hit someone?" Zach asked. "The more I think about it, the less I like it."

"Don't be such a pussy," Jeremy chided.

Zach glared at Jeremy.

"I'm tired of your bullshit, Jeremy," Zach said coldly. "You think this is a game?"

"Kinda, yeah. Life's a game. You got winners and you got losers. I'm gonna be a winner."

"We're all gonna be winners if we do this right," Noah said. "We just need to relax."

"How can we relax cooped up in this place?" Jeremy groused. "At least you get out to go to work."

"He's eatin' better than us, too," Zach said, jokingly.

Noah smiled. Unlike the others, he'd already put his escape plan into motion. While he was supposedly at work, he'd rented a storage unit in which he parked a small rented trailer that he filled with what he wanted from the house. Then he cherry picked items from the other storage unit, things that would be easy to sell or very profitable or necessary, such as flash drives, electronics and tools. His plan was to drop off Zach at the house following the robbery and then hook up the trailer and head north. Driving only during daylight hours he'd eventually make his way to Anchorage. Spending most of his planning efforts on what to bring, he hadn't mapped the route until Tuesday, three days before the op. Looking at Google Maps while at his house, he was dismayed. Most of the route went through Canada. The trip required a passport, which he didn't have and couldn't get by Friday.

He couldn't believe it, sitting in the living room, staring at his laptop, his escape to Alaska ended at the Canadian border. The last thing he wanted to do was to try to cross the border illegally. He'd be paranoid for more than two thousand miles driving across western Canada. Having never been to Canada, he had assumed it was much like the U.S., but as he zoomed in on the map he saw that most of the drive would be through wilderness, with few towns in which to spend the night or buy fuel. It didn't take long for him to admit defeat. He needed another plan.

64

NOAH WASN'T THE ONLY ONE WORKING ON AN ESCAPE plan. Zach, too, planned to dissociate himself from the crew so he could go into business with his girlfriend. But he was having second thoughts. Staying in New Orleans might not be a good idea, especially with Jeremy in the mix. Jeremy was twitchy and quick to take offense. He was a hothead and Zach thought that of the four of them Jeremy was the most likely to be caught. Jeremy craved attention and some-times did stupid things to achieve it. Zach had little doubt that Jeremy would spill his guts if he was caught. Noah had similar misgivings and they discussed what they could do about it.

"Short of killing him, I can't think of anything to shut him up," Noah said gruffly Tuesday evening, still reeling from the dissolution of his escape plan.

"What would you do if you were caught?"

"I don't know. What about you?"

"That's the question, ain't it? It's got me thinking about leaving New Orleans after we're done."

"I'm with you on that."

"Really?"

"Yeah, I'm gonna get outta town."

"Makes sense."

"Where you gonna go?"

"Don't know yet. I was thinking about Alaska but you gotta drive through Canada to get there and I got no passport."

"Gonna disappear in the woods? Become a homesteader or whatever?"

"Yeah, like in those shows. But now I don't even know how to get there."

"You could fly."

"I thought about that, but how do I get the money there?"

"We don't even know how we're gonna get our money. We haven't talked about that. We're not gonna get it right away, are we?"

Noah looked distractedly around the room, as if a solution were written on one of the walls. He was usually all about details but now he'd blown it twice. He'd assumed he could simply drive to Alaska and it had never occurred to ask how they'd get their share from the robbery. Pacing the room for a moment he rummaged through the carry-on bag containing his clothes and pulled out a small pipe and baggie, returning to his chair.

"Wanna toke?" he said, handing the lit pipe to Zach.

"I thought we weren't supposed to smoke dope? It was your rule, right?"

"It was Grizz's but now I'm making a new rule. I need to relax, man. I'm really hyper. This whole thing is starting to get out of hand."

The marijuana had its effect almost immediately. Both men stopped talking for a moment. Zach leaned against the back of his chair and stared at the rust-colored stains on the ceiling. Noah stared across the room, his hand propping up his chin.

"You know, if it weren't for Jeremy, I'd probably stick around," Noah said, breaking the silence.

"When you think about it, yeah, he's the loose cannon. If somebody's gonna fuck up, it's gonna be him and I just don't trust the guy. I never have."

"What can we do about it?"

"Leave town."

Zach changed his position to face Noah.

"You know, Grizz doesn't like him either," Zach said. "You could tell right away."

"I know."

"Maybe he can do something with him, you know, after it's over."

"Like what?"

"Don't fuck with me. You know what."

"You mean like make him disappear."

"Yeah, that's what I mean. Make him disappear. I'll bet it wouldn't be the first time for Grizz. Come to think of it, I'll bet there's bodies buried out where we did the target practice."

"You think?"

"C'mon. These guys are serious fucks," Zach said, shaking his head. "I wonder if they're already thinking about it."

Noah opened his mouth as if to say something, but didn't. Then he shook his head as if to banish a thought.

"What is it?"

Noah sighed, but wouldn't say what was bothering him.

"I wonder if they think we're all like Jeremy?" Zach said.

65

"I'll bet those ARs are a blast to shoot from the hip. What do you think, bro?" Jeremy said as Adan passed a joint to him. Adan smiled while holding his breath. It was Adan's second toke. It was good dope. He didn't need any more.

"And what do you think is under that blanket? Huh?"

Adan shrugged, exhaling a jet of white smoke.

"I dunno."

"I'll bet it's a rocket launcher, what do you think?"

Adan shrugged.

"Or, maybe it's a mortar. Whaddya think?"

"Got no idea. Couldn't tell. I suppose it's something big, else why would they put a blanket over it?"

"Definitely they didn't want us to see it," Jeremy said earnestly. "I guess they don't trust us, huh?"

Adan shrugged.

"Maybe we shouldn't trust them. I mean, we haven't talked about how we're gonna get paid, you know."

"I hadn't thought about that."

"Gotta remember to ask Noah about that," Jeremy said.

"I bet he knows," Adan said.

"Let's go ask him. I heard his van. He's back."

A vacant unit separated Jeremy and Adan from Noah and Zach. High as kites, they bumped into each other as they left their unit.

"Careful, bro," Jeremy said as he knocked on Noah's door.

Noah opened the door a crack and, seeing who was there, opened it halfway.

"What up?"

Jeremy sniffed the air coming out of the room.

"You been smoking weed. I thought there was a rule about that," Jeremy said, giving Adan a sly look.

"Quiet down," Noah said, letting them pass inside while making sure no one from Griswold's crew was watching.

"So it's OK for you to break the rules but not us," Jeremy said with mock indignation after Noah closed the door.

"You caught me. Big deal," Noah said defensively. "I'm just trying to relax after a tough day at the office."

"You got any beer left?"

Noah nodded at Zach who pulled out two cans from the mini fridge. The TV was tuned to a sports channel, the sound off.

"Why don't y'all sit down?" Zach said. "You want a smoke?"

"Naw," Jeremy said with a wave of his hand. "We're already there."

"I kinda figured," Noah said. "What else you doing besides grass?"

"A few pills," Jeremy said. "I was bored."

"Just the marijuana," Adan said. "And the beer."

Taking a generous slug from his can, Jeremy puffed out his cheeks and slowly swallowed.

"Man, that was almost too much. Nearly blew it out my nose."

Noah glanced at Zach, shaking his head.

"I saw that," Jeremy said brusquely, glancing at Adan. "You ain't all that."

Noah shrugged.

"So, did you come here just to visit?"

"Oh, yeah," Jeremy said absently. "We were wondering when we're gonna get paid for this. I mean, when will we see the money?"

"To tell the truth, I don't know," Noah said slowly. "It's something I'm planning to talk to Grizz about tomorrow."

"And why did they take our phones?"

"I don't know."

"You don't know much. You know, I'm lost without my phone, man."

"We all are," Zach agreed.

Noah fidgeted in his chair. He was surprised that Jeremy was having similar misgivings as he'd discussed with Zach. He felt embarrassed for not having locked down the issue of payment before they'd agreed to participate in the op. He'd never done anything like this before and didn't have a handle on it. Perhaps he'd trusted Griswold more than he should have. All of his previous dealings with Griswold were straightforward and uncomplicated. Now that he was working as part of the old man's crew, he felt out of the loop, no longer in control. Vulnerable.

Adan picked up on Noah's discomfort immediately. It was one of the few times he'd seen Noah expressing doubt. As the youngest and least experienced member of the crew, Adan seldom questioned what they did or how they did it.

He had yet to become accustomed to the criminal life and wasn't certain he could pull it off. Turning himself in was still an option that lived in the back of his mind, like suicide.

"So, what do you guys think?" Jeremy asked.

"I wish we hadn't gotten into this," Zach said, anxiously. "This is way over our heads. I didn't realize what we were getting into. I was thinking mostly about the money when we voted."

"You gonna tell Grizz we want out?" Noah asked.

"I feel like we're trapped," Zach said, reaching for the pipe. "I think I could use another toke, man."

66

GRISWOLD COULD SENSE SOMETHING HAD CHANGED when Noah's crew arrived for breakfast. They were uncharacteristically quiet.

"They got the jitters," Horace Bone said as he handed out plates of pancakes.

"Nothing wrong with that," Griswold said. "Is that what it is? You're just nervous about Friday?"

Noah looked at his crew members. No one was smiling.

"We were wondering how we're gonna get paid for this op."

"And why you took our phones," Jeremy interjected.

"That's what's buggin' you, the money and the phones?"

All four nodded in agreement.

"For starters, you'll get paid when I get paid. I'm fronting all the costs and it takes time to move some of this stuff. Any gold we get we can cash out in a day or two. Other stuff might take longer, depending on what we get. You don't think we're gonna cheat you, do you?"

They all shook their heads.

"That's good, because I wouldn't do that. You know that, Noah. We been workin' together long enough you know I don't screw people. It's bad for business. But if you need a few bucks to tide you over until the real money comes in, we can work something out. Would a few thou' for each of you take care of things for now?"

The mood lightened as Griswold whispered something to Ray Gasser who left the room, returning several minutes later with a cash box.

"Will two K do for now?" Griswold said as he counted out four piles of fifty and one hundred dollar bills. Gasser placed a pile in front of each of the young men. Jeremy grabbed his greedily and instinctively counted it, even though he'd watched Griswold do the same. Griswold glanced at Gasser, rolling his eyes.

Adan stared at his pile while the others pocketed theirs.

"You can take it," Griswold said encouragingly. "It's yours. Consider this a small down payment on the biggest score of your lives. You'll get the rest in a week, two at the most. I wanna get paid, too. Whatever we get away with, I won't be sittin' on it."

Seeing the currency took the edge off their nervousness. It was the first tangible evidence that they weren't going to be stiffed. Jeremy was emboldened as he felt the wad of cash in his pants pocket.

"So what about the phones?" he asked.

"You'll get them back when this is over."

"Why not now?"

"'Cause loose lips sink ships," Bone said.

"So, you don't trust us?"

"Ain't you I don't trust," Griswold said. "It's the people you text and call I don't trust. Anyway, you're gonna be real busy from here on out."

67

GRISWOLD HAD AN ENLARGED PHOTOCOPY OF THE floor plan of the imposing, two-story building. Next to it was a printout of an aerial photo of the building and its grounds, which he'd found on the internet. He and Bone had reconnoitered the place several times and liked that it stood by itself with no buildings nearby. The first floor was divided into multiple rooms, including a commercial kitchen and lounge. The upper floor featured a large open area with restrooms. Access was via a broad, carpeted stairway or a smallish elevator near the kitchen. It was Wednesday morning, two days before the op.

"Where is this?" Noah asked.

"Out near Pontchartrain," Griswold said, standing at one end of the table.

"Makes it easy to get in and out," Bone said. "Not like downtown. Plenty of parking."

"We'll drive out there today," Griswold said.

Noah's crew leaned over the table, poring over the photocopies.

"What kinda place is it?"

"They hold fancy weddings and shit there. This week they got what they call the Treasure House. It's invitation only and there's gonna be a lotta gold, Rolexes, jewelry, designer shit, you name it. Friday's some kind of charity auction where the really big bucks will be," Griswold said. "These are the people don't drive their own cars. You know, the one percent of the one percenters."

"What's the layout?"

"We can't be sure, but the way these things usually go is that booths are set up like in a square and the middle is left open so people can walk around. There'll probably be tables and shit so people can sit down and drink or eat or whatever. It starts at seven. I wish I had more on the setup but I don't."

Zach looked at Noah across the table, a wry expression on his face.

"What?" Griswold asked. "You got a question?"

"It sounds like you, we, don't really know how it's set up. I don't like that."

"Neither do I," Griswold growled, "They don't set these things up weeks in advance. I figure that's what they've been doing this week. You got a better idea?"

"Maybe one of us can get inside," Jeremy said.

"How you gonna do that?"

"I don't know. Maybe go out there at night and look through the windows."

"You'd need a big ladder," Bone said. "First floor must be fifteen feet high."

"OK, maybe something else."

"Yeah, why don'cha think about that," Griswold said.

Griswold moved into the kitchen, followed by Bone. They watched the young men as they explored the floor plans and talked about how to get the booth layout. Griswold was impressed enough to nudge Bone.

"I like how they're gettin' into this," Griswold whispered. "I had my doubts but maybe these guys will work out after all."

68

"What I don't get," Noah said after Griswold rejoined them at the table, "is what's gonna stop people from running as soon as we show up. I mean, we got guns and all but we can't just shoot people."

Griswold and Bone exchanged surreptitious smiles.

"We got a secret weapon," Griswold said, as he led them to into the man cave. The lights had been turned up and the doorway into the gunroom was open. Ray Gasser stood near the door like a sentry.

"I got the idea from watching and reading about all those suicide bombers in Iraq and France and places like that," Griswold explained as he led them into the gun room.

"What the fuck is he talking about?" Zach whispered, loud enough for everyone to hear.

"Hear me out," Griswold said, his voice rising. "I got to thinking that what we need is a diversion, something to keep their attention. What better way is there to keep someone's attention than to make them believe you got bombs?"

Noah's crew exchanged looks while Griswold, Gasser and Bone smiled.

"You got bombs?"

Griswold nodded to Bone who lifted the blanket off the pedestal in the center of the room, revealing what looked to be a suicide vest packed with half sticks of dynamite stuffed into pockets. Wires ran from pocket to pocket and throughout the vest. It looked so real that the young men backed away from it, except for Jeremy who leaned forward for a closer look.

"This ain't real, is it?" Jeremy asked.

"It's real," Griswold said, matter-of-factly.

"Can we touch it?"

"Sure, it ain't armed. Doesn't have a battery."

"Will it work, I mean, if you put the battery in would it explode?" Noah asked.

"You can't test these things, you know," Griswold said. "But that ain't what I'm talking about. All that people gotta do is *think* it'll work. Nobody there's gonna have any reason to think it won't. And can you think of anything to get someone's attention that's better than a suicide vest?"

"We tell 'em we got bombs on the stairs and the elevator and anyone tries to use a cell phone might set 'em off," Bone added.

"Who's gonna believe that?"

"They ain't gonna have time to think about it. That's the beauty of this," Griswold said. "They'll back off but they won't be able to take their eyes off the vest. Meanwhile, we grab the good stuff and we're outta there in three minutes."

"Or less," Bone said.

"Quicker the better," Gasser agreed.

Assured that the vest was harmless, Noah's crew touched it, examined it from front to back, whispering among themselves, agreeing that the vest was a brilliant idea. It filled them with confidence and for the time being erased their doubts about the op.

"So who's gonna wear it?" Noah asked.

"One of you guys," Griswold replied, grinning.

69

Noah's crew had a lot to discuss when they met in his room. It was nearly eleven and Noah should have left for his job. The time he'd spent away from the compound he had devoted to preparing his escape from New Orleans but now that was on hold. With only two days left he had to focus his attention on the op.

"I gotta talk to Grizz," he said. "I gotta call in sick."

As he left the room, closing the door behind him, the others agreed that they had two important items to discuss: what they could do to find out how the treasure house would be laid out and who would wear the vest.

Nobody saw Noah as he took several steps toward Griswold's place and stopped. Standing in front of the adjacent room, he stared into the parking lot, biding his time. He did this because of Jeremy's suspicious nature. Even though he'd quit his job, he had to maintain the illusion that he was still working.

"Since it's your idea," Zach said to Jeremy, "how're we gonna get inside the building?"

"I don't know," Jeremy said, annoyed that he had been put on the spot. "Create a distraction. I seen on crime shows that perps'll enter a place dressed like exterminators and say there's an infestation."

"That only works on TV. Someone comes to your place of business and says he's there for this or that. He's gonna know."

"You got a better idea?"

Adan raised his hand, tentatively.

"What?" Jeremy asked, harshly.

Adan pulled his hand down, lowering his head.

"Go ahead, kid. What do ya got?" Zach said, encouragingly.

"The place is for wedding receptions and stuff, right?"

Zach nodded.

"I was thinking maybe me and Jeremy could go out there and say we're getting married and want to see if we want our reception there. You know, get a tour of the place."

Jeremy glared at Adan.

"What the fuck are you saying? I'm not gay, goddammit."

"I know that," Adan said.

"You'd just pretend to be gay," Zach said. "Although, I think you'd make a cute couple."

Jeremy scowled, pushed himself out of his chair and stepped out of the room and onto the walkway, startling Noah who instinctively pretended to be headed toward his room.

"Did you call in sick?"

"Yeah," Noah said. "What're you doing out here?"

"Aw, Adan has some fucking idea about reconning the place."

"That's good."

"Shit it is. He wants me to pretend to be gay. I hate gays as much as I hate nigs. Where does he get an idea like that?"

"You got a better one?"

"I'm workin' on it."

70

JEREMY LIKED THE IDEA OF LEAVING THE COMPOUND. The two thousand bucks were already burning a hole in his pocket and he wanted badly to hook up with a whore. He hated that he couldn't come up with a better idea despite his desperation to do so. But he couldn't think clearly about it. It might have been the pills. Or it might have been that he just wanted to get out of the compound for a few hours no matter what the excuse. They'd have to buy and wear gay clothes. That bothered him. A lot. People would see him. People he didn't know, who would think he was gay. But he couldn't think of anything better. For all he knew Adan was gay. He acted like such a pussy. Never arguing. Quiet. It didn't help that they'd have to tell Griswold about it. One thing he'd decided was that he was damn sure not going to wear the vest.

Griswold laughed when Noah told him about Adan's plan.

"Jeremy says he needs his phone."

"What's he need a phone for?"

"He's gonna video the place. That way we can all see the setup."

"That's a good idea," Griswold said, nodding to Gasser, who left the room, returning shortly with a small box containing four cell phones. Noah selected Jeremy's phone. Gasser held out his hand.

"I'll take it," Gasser said.

"Tell him Ray's going with him. He'll keep them out of trouble."

71

Jeremy balked when Noah told him that Gasser was going to tag along.

"Don't he trust us?"

"What do you think?" Noah said. "What's the harm?"

Jeremy gave Noah a sour look. He'd had plans for his few hours of freedom. Now he was angry. He was so tired of being ordered around, of being told what he could and could not do, that he had half a mind to get in his car and drive away, never to return.

"This whole place is pissing me off," Jeremy snarled. "Can't do this, can't do that. Fuck. We're like prisoners."

"I don't like it any more than you."

"Fuck you," Jeremy shouted. "You get out every fucking day."

"Do not."

"Most days."

Standing in the shade under the second floor overhang in front of Jeremy's room, the door open, the two, one heavily tatted and muscular, the other tatted and scrawny, stared at the broken asphalt parking lot.

"How do we even know you're going to work?" Jeremy asked, defiantly.

"You think I'm lying?" Noah said, scornfully, pressing closer to his accuser. "Is that what you think?"

Jeremy knew that Noah could knock him unconscious with one punch. As quick to anger as he was, he was also deeply into self-preservation. He only engaged in unfair fights, which usually meant watching someone else get beat up and getting the last lick in when the victim was already down. Or drunks. Rolling drunks was easy. Didn't even need an escape route with them.

"Do I get my phone?"

Common sense had overcome his temper. Noah told him he didn't have the phone just as Gasser approached.

"Where's the little guy?" Gasser asked.

"Hey, Adan, time to go," Jeremy shouted.

The three of them walked in silence toward Jeremy's Prius when Gasser veered off course.

"Where you going?"

"We ain't takin' your car," Gasser said. "I got one in the back. It's bigger and got more horses."

With Gasser leading the way, Jeremy followed, his mind clouded by rage. Nothing was working out the way he'd thought it should. Noah pissed him off. Gasser pissed him off. Everything pissed him off. And he had no outlet to vent. No one to pick on, except his roommate.

"This is shit," he muttered to Adan, who wasn't annoyed by the situation, wasn't aware that Jeremy was upset, wasn't responding the way Jeremy had hoped.

"C'mon, man. They're using us. Can't you see that? And it's all because of you and your fucking gay idea. Where did that come from, anyway? Who thinks like that?"

"Don't get mad at me, man," Adan said. "I'm not the one in charge."

Problem was that Jeremy couldn't express his anger to the one in charge. Griswold would crush him like a bug. Gasser and Bone were no different. Neither Noah or Zach wanted Jeremy as their roommate and Adan had no choice in the matter. He was the odd man out.

72

With Gasser driving the black Crown Victoria, they left the compound. Jeremy rode shotgun while Adan sat by himself in the back.

"Can I have my cell phone?"

"When we get there," Gasser said. "Where you wanna buy your outfits?"

Jeremy smiled crookedly. Staring out the tinted window, he struggled to control his resentment. He couldn't think straight. All he wanted to do was to get out of the car and run. But there was nothing he could do. He wished he hadn't left Adan's gun in the room. Even if he didn't use it, it would make him feel better. Make him feel like he was in control.

"I don't know," Jeremy said. "Where do you buy your clothes?"

He realized immediately his mistake. The right arm swung across his throat like a fence post, pinning him against the seat back, his hands shooting up to his throat as if trying to keep his head from popping off. Gasser withdrew his arm quickly, never taking his eyes off the road.

"Don't be mouthin' off to me, shithead," Gasser scolded.

Adan couldn't see what had happened but realized something was wrong. Jeremy was gasping for air. Turning onto a residential street, Gasser pulled alongside the curb and, with the motor running, looked at Jeremy. He wondered if he'd hit him too hard, maybe crushed his windpipe. Were that the case he'd have no choice but to finish him off. He couldn't take him to an emergency room. He'd be sure to turn them in. It hadn't been his intention to inflict permanent damage. It was just that he didn't take insults from punks.

"You OK?" Gasser asked quietly. "You need to go to the hospital?"

Momentarily unable to speak, Jeremy waved his hand as if to say no.

"That's good," Gasser said. "I didn't mean to hit you hard."

It took a minute, but Jeremy recovered quickly enough to offer a verbal defense.

"I didn't mean nothing by it," he said, raising his head, his voice unsteady. "I was just asking. Shit, I thought I was dying."

"Bullshit," Gasser said. "You know what you meant and so do I. You might get away with being a wise guy with people your own age, but don't try it with people like me. Got that? Now, where you wanna go?"

Motivated by a brief introduction to his own mortality, Jeremy found the germ of a new idea, one so obvious that he couldn't believe he hadn't thought of it. Perhaps his mind had been working on it as soon as Adan suggested they pretend to be gay, looking for a way out of it, any way out.

"Fuck the clothes," he said, hoarsely. "Let's just go out there."

"And do what?"

"You'll see."

"That ain't good enough. Boss says you was gonna pretend to be a couple."

"I changed my mind."

"Boss won't like that."

"Then you fucking dress up and go do it."

Gasser raised his arm threateningly.

"Look, boy, I don't fuck around. You think you gonna push me around. Forget it while you still can."

"I got a better plan."

"What's that?"

"Most places when they ain't open don't have security people so I figure I'm gonna run in, run up the stairs, do the video, take maybe five, ten seconds and run out. We'll be outta there before anyone knows what happened."

Gasser thought about it momentarily and then nodded approvingly. For him, it was all about getting the job done as efficiently and cleanly as possible. Griswold could care less how he did it.

"You shudda thought that the first time. But OK. I wasn't looking forward to watching you guys play dress up anyway."

As they pulled away from the curb, Jeremy straightened himself and glanced back at Adan, winking confidently.

"Can I have my phone now?"

Greedily accepting it from Gasser, Jeremy immediately checked his messages and calls. There were none.

"Hey, what is this?" he said, dismayed. "It ain't working."

Gasser smiled.

"Grizz took the card out."

73

GRISWOLD GOT A CHUCKLE FROM GASSER'S ACCOUNT of how Jeremy got the video of the venue's upstairs layout. At normal speed, the video quality was uneven, herky-jerky, patchy lighting, not quite nauseating. At a slower speed, it was good enough for their purposes. It showed booths and display tables and rows of seating in the center of the room facing a low, temporary stage with a lectern.

"Gotta say, the kid's got balls," Gasser said as they watched Jeremy's video in the theater room. "In and out like he said."

"This is better than I hoped," Griswold said, watching the video in slow-motion on the flat screen.

"I've seen better," Bone said.

"I mean the layout. Looks like people will be sitting ducks."

"They won't know what hit 'em," Gasser said.

"That's where they're holding the auction," Griswold said.

"What are they going to auction?"

"Doesn't matter. With these people it's all good."

"What about the booths?"

"I don't know. Jewelry. Gold. Coins. Whatever."

"Like a flea market for rich people?" Bone suggested.

"That's a good one," Griswold said. "Anyway, we don't have to get it all. We only have a couple minutes so go for the easy stuff. The wallets, watches and 'specially the women's jewelry."

"I count six rows of seven chairs," Bone said.

"How many chairs is that?" Gasser said.

"Forty two," Griswold said. "Figure half men, half women. That's a bunch of expensive watches, and the women will be wearing their best stuff to impress each other. Hell, we might not even have to look at the booths."

"We want their cell phones?"

"Hell, no. Nothing electronic. Don't want them tracking us."

"And wallets?"

"Any cash they're carrying. Probably won't be much," Griswold said. "Rings, earrings, anything the women are wearing. That's where the money is."

"Think we'll get a million?"

"Let's hope," Griswold said.

74

JEREMY COULDN'T STOP TALKING ABOUT WHAT HE'D done, describing it in detail, leaving out the part where Gasser hit him across the throat. They were in Noah's room. Jeremy wanted to light a pipe, have a beer, anything, but Noah wouldn't let him. Griswold wanted to meet with them after he had time to study the video.

"It was like in the movies," Jeremy said. "I was nervous but not scared. I had my camera app loaded when they dropped me off down the road so I walked on this little dirt path until I got to the side of the house. I saw a couple cameras so I pulled my hat down and kinda scrunched over till I got to the steps. But the cameras prolly weren't working 'cause why would they that time of day with no one around?"

"What did you do then?" Zach asked.

"Right then and there I thought, what if the door is locked, you know, what do I do?"

"Hadn't thought of that before?"

"We figured the place would be open, you know, like a normal day doing normal stuff. Why would they lock the door? But it's different when you're there, you know, alone and not being sure."

"Where was Adan?"

"We drove around for a few minutes," Adan said.

Not wanting to share the moment, Jeremy described how he slowly turned the door knob with his right hand, pressing gently to make sure the door would open, taking out his cell phone with his left.

"I took a deep breath like I was starting a race and just like that I pushed the door open and walked into this lobby like it was a normal thing to do. I don't know what I was expecting, but it was empty. I heard talking somewhere downstairs. The stairway was on the left. Big, wide sucker with thick carpet. I ran up that sucker and didn't make a sound."

Pausing for effect, Jeremy saw that his companions hung on every word. It was his time to shine.

"Then what?" Zach asked.

Jeremy smiled, raising his eyebrows.

"Well, my friend, there was this giant room in front of me, all laid out like for a party. I did a pan of the entire room and then the sides and the middle, even the ceiling. I even got the floor. And I got it all in like thirty seconds, which is twice as long as I thought I'd do but nobody was there. It was just this big room with these big windows."

"Did anyone see you?"

"That's the best part. I didn't see nobody, and I was looking. But I didn't run down the stairs like I did on the way up. Didn't want to fall. And when I got to the lobby I just let myself out, not letting the door slam, and once I got off the porch I ran like hell. The rest, as they say, is history."

Jeremy beamed with pride, watching for reactions from his audience.

"Did you see the video?" Noah asked.

"I tried but it was hard to do in the car."

"He was getting car sick," Adan said.

"Was not," Jeremy replied heatedly.

"You said—"

"I didn't say nothin'."

Jeremy's smile vanished.

"Doesn't matter," Noah said. "We'll see it soon enough."

75

"Why you say something like that?" Jeremy asked Adan after they left Noah's room.

"Say what?"

"That I got car sick."

"You said it," Adan protested.

"Doesn't mean you should repeat it. Makes me look bad."

Adan sighed. Sometimes he didn't know what to say to Jeremy. Sometimes the littlest things would set him off. He was friendly when he wanted to be but he was something else when he wasn't. Adan couldn't figure him out. One day he felt he could trust him as a friend and the next something someone said, it didn't even have to be Adan, would set him off and Adan would be in the middle of it by virtue of being his roommate and the only one of the three who had not yet decided not to trust him. But he was learning.

"At least you didn't tell them about that fuck Gasser blindsiding me," Jeremy said, softening. "It was a sucker punch all the way."

"You know," Adan said, "sometimes you act like my friend and other times you act like you're not."

"What's that s'posed to mean?"

Never one to start a confrontation, except once, Adan noticed that Jeremy tended to back down from arguments with Noah and Zach. When he was angry about something, he didn't take it out on them. But Adan felt his emotions rising. He trembled. He felt hot, much like he did when he shot the bully.

"It means, I don't know what to expect from you and if you don't start treating me better—"

"You'll what?" Jeremy said menacingly.

Adan looked away, his head bowed.

"You know, I like you, Adan. It's just that sometimes you piss me off."

76

Only one decision remained for Noah's crew before the op.

"We need to decide who's going to wear the vest."

"Why don't you wear it?" Jeremy said.

"It's not like it's gonna be armed," Noah said.

"Then, why don't you wear it?"

"Why don't you?"

"I already did my bit, remember. It's someone else's turn."

Griswold had assured Noah that it couldn't explode without attaching a battery to the wiring harness and then using either a remote switch or a triggering mechanism deployed by the wearer. They had examined it closely in the gun room and they could see the empty, nine-volt battery connector dangling from the bottom and the push-button trigger.

"Grizz said he doesn't even know if it will work," Noah said. "And we're not going to find out. People see the vest they ain't gonna put up any resistance. We just tell them to shut up, hand over their stuff and we're gone. It'll probably be the most money any of us make in our whole lives."

"And then we split up and never see each other again?" Jeremy asked.

"That's the plan."

"What about the radios and all the other shit?"

"Bad timing. We'll work something out."

Jeremy shook his head. Although he hadn't thought about the storage unit since he and Adan had last visited it, he was suddenly interested.

"That's bullshit," he said. "We took all those risks to get everything and now it's like we don't care about it?"

"We're gonna make enough money off this one op to start over, man," Zach said. "Y'all already know I'm going straight after this and, really, I don't care what happens to the radios or anything else. I just want to get this over with."

Jeremy didn't trust Noah, or Zach, or anybody. It was his nature and he never questioned it. But he knew where Noah and Zach stood. Even if they voted on what to do with the storage unit, the best he could hope for was a tie. But he didn't have a plan for what to do after the op. His strength was breaking and entering. Noah's strength was in getting rid of the stuff they stole. It had worked well but now they were going big time. While they were part of it, it was Griswold's op. Noah and his crew were little more than muscle. Their function was to intimidate the rich saps for a few minutes and then escape. What followed was a blank slate to Jeremy. He had fantasies of how he'd spend his loot. Fancy hotels. Hookers in silk dresses. Top shelf liquor. Maybe a sidekick like Adan to do his bidding. The kid was a wimp but he could follow orders and that was enough for Jeremy.

"Why don't we draw straws?" Zach suggested.

"Not me," Jeremy said firmly.

"OK. The three of us," Noah said. "That OK with you, Adan?"

Adan had tuned out the back and forth between Jeremy and Noah. It seemed to him that all that Jeremy ever did was squabble with whomever he was with. He hated it. He wanted everyone to get along, but he didn't have a plan for what he would do after the op either, what he would do with the money. He would have liked the crew to stay together but it was clear Zach would be gone and so would Noah. He didn't like the idea of staying with Jeremy but he was the only other person he could call a friend in New Orleans, and he had a car. He was afraid that if he didn't follow somebody, he'd become lost.

"I wish y'all would stop arguing," Adan said, exasperated. "I'll wear the vest."

77

After reviewing Jeremy's video and screen captures of the layout, everyone gathered around the dining table to hear Griswold present the final plan for the op.

"It's pretty much what I expected," he started. "We didn't know where they'd set up the chairs but it makes sense to do it in the middle of the room. Thanks to Jeremy, we now know it."

Jeremy smiled, his eyes darting to see how the others reacted.

Griswold held up a marked up screen capture.

"See the circles? That's where you're gonna put the bombs."

"Bombs?" Zach asked incredulously. "What kinda bombs?"

"Fake bombs. Everybody's gonna be watching the auction when we bust in so we don't have to worry about someone gettin' in the way."

"What about security? Won't there be security?"

"Rent-a-cops," he said dismissively. "Besides, they won't be expectin' nothin' so we can take them by surprise. Bone will take care of downstairs. You point a shotgun at someone and it makes them think. Even off-duty cops."

"But what if they do something?" Zach asked urgently.

"Let us worry about that. We'll take care of it. You guys just focus on your job, which is to put the bombs out and collect the valuables."

"Something I don't understand," Zach said. "Why do we need the vest? I mean, it's not like one of us is going to blow himself up."

"Way ahead of you there," Griswold said. "Adan's gonna act like a hostage. We'll push him around and I'll say we picked him up off the street and I'll show them a remote."

"I still don't get why they'd think we'd blow up the vest. Wouldn't it kill us, too?"

"If they got time to think about it. But they won't. We'll be in and out before they know what happened. All they're gonna see is the guy with the vest. They won't put two and two together till we're long gone. These are very rich people. They ain't gonna put up a fight. What's money to them? They'll be scared shitless. They can always get more money but they can't get another life."

Griswold had an answer for everything. Bone and Gasser knew everything already and would rather have been doing something else, but Griswold had insisted they be part of the meeting. He wanted everyone to see that they were on the same team. After the questions had dried up and he'd finished his presentation, he met individually with each of Noah's crew to confirm that they'd been listening and that they knew their roles. As they left for their rooms, Griswold took Adan aside.

"You guys go ahead," Griswold said. "I just need to say a few things to our hostage."

78

"YOU'RE THE STAR OF THE SHOW," GRISWOLD SAID AS they sat on one of the sofas in the conversation pit. "People are gonna be watchin' you the whole time. You gotta look scared, really scared, like you're afraid of dying. But don't say nothin'. Cry if you can, you know, tears. If I say something to you, like I threaten you or something, react like it's real. You only got to do this for a few minutes and it'll be over. Can you do that?"

A serious look on his face, staring at his knees, Adan nodded slightly.

"If you don't mind my asking, I thought we were gonna wear masks."

"We are, but you aren't. You're a hostage, remember."

"So, people will see me?"

"They won't be paying attention to your face. Just keep your head down and the cameras won't see you."

Griswold eyed Adan momentarily. The youth looked away.

"So, as I understand it, you shot somebody at your school. Is that right?"

"Yes, sir, but it was a mistake."

Adan explained how the shooting had happened. It was clear from his tone that he was still remorseful.

"What about your parents?"

"My dad's in prison and I never knew my mom."

"So who raised you?"

"My gramps."

Griswold shook his head after Adan explained how his father wound up in prison.

"Goddamn," Griswold said. "Things just haven't gone your way, have they?"

"No sir."

"Tell you what, that's gonna change starting Friday."

Adan smiled.

79

IT WAS PIZZA ALL AROUND THURSDAY EVENING. Griswold let them have one beer each. While the young men were enjoying themselves, Gasser and Bone drove to New Orleans where Gasser boosted a late model black Chevy Suburban with dark tinted windows. For good measure, he stole a license plate from a Honda parked in an alley.

"Don't want anyone hungover in the morning," Griswold told the young men before shutting the door on his theater room.

Everyone knew his role. Sitting around the table, Noah's crew tried on their latex masks, depicting zombies and scary clowns. Each of them would wear a gimme cap, dark blue coveralls and nitrile gloves. Nothing about them would be exposed. Friday they would make a half dozen military surplus shoulder bags look like bombs, which they would do by exposing a wire here and there with a brick for heft. Nothing sophisticated, just something to get the audience's imagination going.

Adan watched wistfully as his companions played

around with their masks, trying to scare each other like children. When Zach asked where his mask was, Adan shrugged.

"I don't get one. I'm the hostage."

"That sucks," Jeremy said, still wearing his mask, holding his arms out like a zombie.

"That's not fair," Zach said, looking at Noah.

"Wasn't my decision," Noah said.

"There's cameras, you know," Zach said.

"Do you want to be the hostage?"

Zach shook his head.

"I'm not even sure I want to be here."

Removing his mask, Jeremy slapped it on the table.

"It's a little late for that, bro, don't you think?" he said.

"Fuck you, Jeremy," Zach said angrily.

The two glared at each other.

"Knock it off," Noah said. "I'll ask Grizz about it in the morning. I don't want to disturb him right now."

Jeremy smiled and nodded.

"I'm all right with it," Adan said unconvincingly.

"You volunteered," Jeremy asserted.

"I know. I didn't think about the cameras. I've never done anything like this before."

"None of us has, kid," Zach said.

80

Nobody from Noah's crew slept well Thursday night, Noah especially. He'd gone over Griswold's plan front and back and couldn't find a flaw. It was more sophisticated than anything he would ever think of doing. He seemed to have an answer for everything. Except one. What happens to Adan? What was the plan for Adan?

He recalled the conversation he'd had with Griswold about Adan and that he was a fugitive. He'd thought he was just another homeless kid. Learning that he was a fugitive alarmed him. Although he never said it in so many words, Griswold seemed willing to take care of his problem in a way that Noah couldn't. But that seemed so long ago. He liked Adan a lot more than Jeremy. If anything, he could do without Jeremy, though he could also do without Adan, or anyone else for that matter.

"You up?" he whispered.

"Can't fall asleep," Zach said. "The dope's not doing it for me. Wish I had sleeping pills."

"Me too."

Noah sat on the edge of his bed, looking across the darkness toward Zach's bed. Moments passed, his mind not one hundred percent awake, not sure if talking would help him get over his anxiety.

"What do you think is gonna happen tomorrow?"

"I don't know. I wish I did."

"You think it'll work?"

"Sounds like it. Either that or Grizz did a really good sales job. I can't tell anymore."

"What do you think about Adan?"

"What about Adan?"

"Not wearing a mask. That bugs me."

"Well, it makes sense the way Grizz explained it. I mean, if you're gonna wear a suicide vest—"

"That's the thing. Do we really need it with the bombs and all?"

Noah could hear Zach sigh and adjust his position so that he sat on the edge of his bed, facing him. They spoke quietly, as if someone in the room was asleep.

"What difference does it make? He's not gonna change the plan at the last minute."

"I know, I just wonder. You know, I feel bad about talking to him about Adan, you know, when I told him he was wanted in Texas. I thought, holy shit, there could be a fugitive task force looking for him. I mean, shooting a kid in school is one of those things they don't give up on."

"You thought he was a threat," Zach said sympathetically.

"Yeah, to all of us. We got no way of knowing. But, you know, he's a nice kid. I like him. He's like somebody's little brother. But I just can't figure out what's gonna happen to him. I mean, what's Grizz gonna do?"

"You gonna ask him?"

"I said I would but I don't know now. I don't know if I want to know."

81

GRISWOLD HAD TOLD NOAH THAT GASSER AND BONE needed to use his van. It was early Friday morning. Noah asked for an explanation.

"Y'all aren't gonna be living there no more."

Noah was dumbfounded.

"What? Why? Where will we live?"

"I got another place for you in Hammond. That's where they're taking your stuff. It's a bigger place. You'll like it. Anyway, it's a done deal. I don't want you around after this goes down."

"How are we gonna get our shares?"

"We'll meet up at my place after. I'm not saying you gotta go immediately. You can stay here until we work things out. Shouldn't take long. Don't worry about getting paid. You'll get your shares."

Noah had a problem with Griswold's plan but realized it would be pointless to argue.

"I know you're upset about this but for now don't tell your crew. They don't need to know right now. It'll just screw things up. That Jeremy kid could make a problem for us, you understand?"

Noah understood, staring at Griswold with a stone face. This was so out of left field.

"Couldn't you have said something before? We could've packed up, made sure—"

"Your stuff'll be OK. Anyway, you'll be rolling in money. Hell, most of the stuff is shit anyway. I been there. Couldn't give it away."

Griswold put his arm around Noah's shoulder, speaking in confidential tones.

"You're the leader of your guys. You gotta put this behind you for now, focus on tonight. After that, you don't like what I done, we'll talk about it. Shit, I'm not even gonna charge you rent the first month."

Noah smiled through a frown. Hammond was an hour's drive northwest of New Orleans, near the intersection of two interstates, one of which would be his escape route, which he could take all the way to St. Louis.

"I didn't want to do this but, you know, the heat'll be on and I'm just taking precautions. You can understand that, right?"

Noah nodded. He'd taken precautions as well, pilfering from his crew's storage unit to help his escape to Alaska, or wherever. Conscious of his own guilt, he didn't press Griswold over what would otherwise have been an intolerable act. He'd been through Hammond several times but never found a reason to stop. It was one of those towns with nothing going on. That could work in their favor.

"So, they're clearing out the house?"

"Everything. Nobody'll ever know you lived there, 'cept the neighbors."

"We didn't have anything to do with them."

"That's good," Griswold said, eyeing Noah attentively. "We're good then, right? You won't say anything till after it's over?"

"I'll keep it to myself. Anyway, I think everyone's gonna split as far as they can. Probably just go to Hammond to get our stuff and be on our separate ways."

"Whatever works for you."

82

GRISWOLD DID EVERYTHING HE COULD TO KEEP NOAH'S crew busy Friday. They went over everything several times, rehearsed what they would do and how they would do it. They'd drive out in two cars. Noah and his crew would use the stolen Chevy with the stolen plate while Griswold and his crew would drive the Expedition. They'd drive out together, Griswold in the lead, his car's trunk filled with weapons, the fake bombs, vest and the canvas shoulder bags they'd use to carry the loot. They expected to fill them with small, expensive items, leaving larger items behind.

"Leave your wallets and any ID behind. No jewelry. No earrings. Nothing."

"Why we gotta do that?" Jeremy asked.

"'Cause if you drop something, leave something behind, they might be able to use it to identify us. It don't take much. Y'all got fingerprints on file just like us. And maybe DNA. I don't know, I don't care. But nowadays they can get DNA off a earring, hair, anything."

"That's why we're wearing masks and wigs and shit," Bone said.

"You know, hair falls out all the time."

"There's dozens of people there and who knows how many people go through that place in a week?" Griswold said. "Any hair we leave behind is gonna have company. If I thought that was a problem you'd have shaved heads. Bone'll shave you if you want."

"OK, OK," Noah said. "No ID. Got it. But what about a driver's license?"

Griswold rolled his eyes.

"Man, are you not listening? No ID. None. Nada."

It was the first time Griswold spoke harshly to Noah in the presence of his crew. Though they said nothing, it was not lost on them. Griswold was the boss.

83

Noah and Zach were in the front, Adan and Jeremy in the rear. Noah kept a healthy distance behind Griswold's car as they took what seemed to him a circuitous route toward their destination. Everyone was nervous, quiet, introspective. Time didn't exist for them as they struggled to tamp down the adrenaline rushing through their veins. This was like nothing they'd ever done. Zach remained wary and uncertain whether he was fully committed. Noah focused on driving, making sure to signal turns, not do anything that would cause someone to take notice. Jeremy took deep breaths, nudging Adan who stared out the window.

"How you feel?" he whispered.

"Fine. Nervous."

"I'm not nervous," Jeremy boasted. "Just kinda excited, you know. You'll be OK. You'll see. Soon as we get there."

It was dark when they'd left the compound. Griswold had allowed twenty minutes for the drive but Friday traffic was slowing them down. The parking lot at the plantation was filled with luxury cars and limousines, with drivers mingling and using cellphones.

"Shit," Griswold said, "I didn't think of this," as they drove by, turning back toward town.

The parking lot was set at a distance from the two-story building. It was a good thing it was dark. They were just two cars on a public road.

"What are we gonna do, boss?" Bone asked. "Those kids are prolly wondering what the fuck is going on."

"Yeah, I shoulda let Noah have a phone. Shit. We gotta stop somewhere."

84

"WHAT THE FUCK IS GOING ON?" ZACH SAID, AS THEY followed Griswold's car past the house. "Why don't we pull in?"

"I don't know," Noah said, nervously, gripping the steering wheel tightly, following Griswold's car closely. Out of sight of the building, they drove another mile before Griswold turned off on a side street, pulling over in the darkness between two widely spaced street lamps. Gasser, who sat in the front passenger seat, rolled down his window and waved his arm.

"What's he doing?" Zach said, squinting into the darkness.

"He wants us to go to him," Noah said. "Go, Zach. See what's going on."

"This don't feel right," Jeremy said anxiously. "Something's going on. They're setting us up."

"What are you talking about?" Noah said sternly.

"That's why I brought this," Jeremy said, holding up Adan's pistol. "I just knew they were up to something."

"They're not up to anything," Noah said. "Put that thing away, for chrissake. What's the matter with you?"

"You ain't the boss," Jeremy said coldly. "Not anymore."

While Noah and Jeremy bickered, Zach crouched beside the front passenger door of Griswold's car.

"Who are you?" Griswold asked.

"Zach. Noah told me to come. What's going on?"

"Too many cars in the lot. We got a change of plans. We'll go around and park in the turning circle in front of the place. Got it? Everything else is the same."

Zach barely got back into the car before Griswold pulled onto the road. He described what had happened as Noah closely followed Griswold. Jeremy wasn't buying it.

"This is fucked, I'm tellin' you," Jeremy said. "After all that planning and he misses something like this. Explain that."

"Shit happens," Zach said.

"Besides, he needs us as much as we need him," Noah said. "Without us—"

"They'd get someone else," Jeremy said quickly.

"He didn't have time. It was us or nothing. Just cool it. Everybody, just cool it. We'll do this the way we planned it. If you can't do this, just stay in the car."

"Fuck that," Jeremy said angrily. "You ain't cutting me out of what's mine."

85

JEREMY AND ZACH WERE ALREADY OUT OF THEIR vehicle as Noah put the Suburban into park, their masks, wigs, caps and gloves in place. In seconds they crowded behind the Griswold's car as Gasser handed out the gear. Griswold helped Adan into the vest.

"Just remember, you're not one of us. You're a hostage. You got that?"

"Yes, sir," Adan said quietly, pulling a cap low over his head. "Is it OK if I just keep my head down?"

"That's fine. Just make sure you look scared. I might push you around a little, but don't take it personal. It's just part of the act, like I told you."

Adan smiled slightly in the yellow light of the porch that filtered onto the brick drive. In his haste, Jeremy nearly tripped going up the porch stairs, as they converged on the doorway with the obese Bone bringing up the rear, breathing heavily.

"OK," Griswold whispered to Noah and Zach, who stood in front of the ornate double doors, "open 'em slow. We don't wanna barge in. No commotion."

Noah and Zach nodded slightly at each other and slowly proceeded into the high-ceilinged lobby with its huge, brightly lit chandelier. Within seconds, all seven were inside as they closed the doors quietly. People were talking loudly amongst the banging and clanging in the kitchen area. They could hear someone speaking loudly upstairs but couldn't make out what he was saying. Griswold nodded to Bone who, sawed-off shotgun in hand, stepped toward the kitchen while Griswold directed Gasser to lead the way up the thickly carpeted, curved stairway to the second floor.

The stairway opened directly into an immense, high-ceilinged room. The perimeter was dark with light concentrated in the center where fashionably dressed people sat in rows facing a man who was taking bids on an item that he held in a raised hand. While the majority of people were participating in the auction, others milled about or had positioned themselves in booths lined up on either side of the auction area.

Griswold was the first to burst the bubble on the auction, his left hand on the back of Adan's neck, as he paraded the teenager to the front of the room where the light was brightest and the vest could be seen for what it was. Several people gasped as Noah, Jeremy and Zach distributed fake bombs just near the phalanx of seated bidders. Gasser remained at the stairway landing, shotgun in hand, ready to discourage runners.

"Everybody shut the fuck up," Griswold barked, holding up a remote and pointing at Adan whom he instructed to move to one side. "Those bags, they're bombs just like that kid is wearing. Your cellphones could set them off. We don't want to hurt you. We just want your money and your valuables. Just go ahead and put your stuff in the bags. Just drop it in like you're giving out Halloween candy and we'll be outta here in no time. Give us shit and some of you might end up dead. I know you got insurance so if your fucking watch is worth your life then go ahead, be a hero. We got ARs and shotguns and when we shoot we won't be aiming. Got it?"

A grim silence settled over the room, with only the sound of Noah's crew shuffling silently among their victims, holding out their shoulder bags. Some of the women threw their purses in. Men did the same with their wallets. Most of them couldn't keep their eyes off Adan, who represented the existential threat that Griswold predicted. Filled with fear, they weren't able to see the unlikelihood that the robbers would detonate a bomb that would kill them as well as their victims. Sensing his opportunity, Griswold directed Gasser to grab whatever he could from the booths on one side of the auction area while he filled his shoulder bag with items from the facing side. In four minutes, he signaled for his men, including Adan, to step to the back of the room while he stood in the front, watching.

"We're leaving now. You wanna be brave and use your phone, well, if you're unlucky and it sets off a bomb, everyone who dies is on you. Got it?"

With a nod, the others quickly descended the stairs where they met Bone, who had deposited his bomb in the kitchen and had instructed the kitchen help and the two security guards in the same manner as Griswold had instructed his victims.

"Any trouble?" Griswold asked as he and Bone stepped onto the porch, facing the open entrance and pausing momentarily to see if anyone was following.

"Piece of cake, Boss."

Moving quickly toward the cars, removing their disguises hastily, Griswold's crew worked with practiced efficiency while Noah's group acted as if they'd just won a football game with fist bumps and loud talking.

"Goddamn! I thought I was gonna suffocate," Jeremy said as he tossed his mask into the back seat of the Suburban, while Noah opened the hatch.

"Shut up," Griswold said. "We're not done yet. Put your weapons and bags in my car."

"What does he mean, we're not done yet?" Jeremy asked Noah.

"Just do what the boss says, asshole" Bone said, while Griswold, standing in the darkness behind Noah's car, helped Adan out of the vest, handing it gingerly to Gasser, who laid it in the back of Noah's vehicle, fiddling with it for a moment before closing the hatch.

"Why does he talk to me like that?" Jeremy asked bitterly.

"I don't know," Noah whispered. "Maybe he doesn't like you."

"Put your stuff in the boss's car," Bone said insistently. "C'mon, let's get going. Time's a wastin'."

Jeremy was the last to part with his shoulder bag. It was as if someone had taken away his Christmas gifts. Griswold thought they were going too slow. He took Noah aside.

"There's a change of plans. You don't follow me out. We go one way, you go the other. We'll meet up at the house."

"But—"

"No buts, kid. I ain't asking your opinion. Just do it."

Noah nodded solemnly. He, Jeremy and Zach hopped quickly into the Suburban.

"Where's Adan?" Jeremy asked.

"I don't know," Noah said, looking into the back seat. "I thought he was with you."

"Let's get going," Zach said urgently. "Grizz put him in his car. I just saw him do it."

"Why would he do that?" Jeremy asked.

"I don't know."

Noah thought back to when he'd told Griswold about the fugitive who was living with him. He wondered whether Griswold planned to dispose of the teenager. He thought about mentioning it but Zach punched him lightly in the shoulder to get a move on.

Noah took a right at the end of the drive and Griswold took a left.

"Did you get the battery in?"

"Yeah," Gasser said, riding shotgun. Griswold handed him the remote.

"Do you think this will work?" Bone asked as the two cars moved apart. He sat in the back seat with Adan, who leaned against the side window, sensing that something bad was about to happen but unable to do anything about it, and stared at his reflection in the glass.

"Only one way to find out," Gasser said, looking out the back window at a point of red light in the distance.

"You better do it now or they'll be out of range," Griswold said.

Pointing the remote toward the rear window as if changing TV channels, Gasser pressed the button once. A second passed and then the red light disappeared, swallowed by a distant ball of flame that briefly lit up the interior of Griswold's car.

"Well, that's that," Bone said, looking at Adan.

THE END

Sign up for the free newsletter to receive updates & discounts on John Koloen's latest books at watchfirepress.com/jk.

INSECTS (EXCERPT)

A deadly carnivorous insect.

A scientific expedition trapped in the uncharted Brazilian rainforest.

One horror filled night.

Entomologist Howard Duncan has a generous grant and a wealthy lover. Now he's on the verge of a find in the Brazilian rainforest that will reenergize his career: the rarely sighted reptilus blaberus, an insect like no other.

But something has changed - nature has started producing an antidote to the fungal infection that previously held the insect population in check. Skeletons provide Duncan and his team with an ominous first clue about the potential consequences.

And as the hunters become the hunted, the team must fight for their lives if they want to survive the terror-filled night.

1

ON THE STREET BELOW THE APARTMENT BUILDING ON
Avenue 7 de Setembro, several cars came to a screeching
halt, followed by angry shouts in Portuguese and a brief
honking of horns. Howard Duncan paid no attention,
despite the open windows of his third-floor apartment overlooking the steamy, wet street below. Sweat dripping from
his brow, he stared at the 15-inch laptop, his face inches
from the LCD. Nearsighted, he'd removed his stylish horn
rims to get a better look at the digital images but found only
frustration. What he wanted was a big color print that he
could examine under a magnifying glass, or a giant flat
screen.

Frustration increased faster than the humidity. He felt
his blood pressure rising, and left the small table in the
kitchenette to pace through the two rooms that he shared
with his assistant Cody Boyd. They were in Manaus to
survey insects in the Rio Negro basin to fulfill the terms of
Duncan's grant, which he hoped would lead to a multi-year
renewal or at least an extension. Like any graduate entomol-

ogist, Boyd hoped to discover a previously unidentified species that would launch his career.

"Did you see that?" Boyd shouted as he burst into the tiny apartment, nearly crashing into Duncan. He'd run up the three flights and had to catch his breath.

"See what?"

"I almost got hit by a jerk in a Fiat. I had the right-of-way, goddammit. I was lucky I didn't drop the food," Boyd said, holding out a plastic bag. "I got Brasileiroas and a couple pastels we can have now or later."

Duncan acknowledged Boyd but continued pacing.

"They're still warm," Boyd said as he emptied the bag on the small table, pushing the laptop aside and pouring a cup of coffee from the French press on the small counter-top. The coffee was tepid. He reheated it in the small microwave and asked Duncan if he wanted a cup.

Duncan approached Boyd from behind and, leaning against the back of Boyd's chair, said gruffly, "I can't tell a damn thing from your pictures. They're a little blurry, and I don't have a clue about their size. It would have been helpful if you'd put a ruler in the picture."

Boyd sighed, having taken a bite from his buttered Brasileiroas roll. He had hoped to savor his breakfast in peace, but that was no longer possible.

Boyd had photographed the insects on a day trip some fifty miles from the office. He'd gone with a local guide on a boat to a narrow peninsula that jutted into the river like a jetty. He'd had no particular reason for stopping there other than it provided an easy landing and because it was piled with driftwood and seemed promising. The insects were hidden under a pile of brush, and he was startled when he exposed them. They reminded him of cockroaches but were larger and shaped somewhat like a .50-caliber bullet. He ran off a series of photos using autofocus and autoexposure and then tried to pick one of the insects up with his bare hands. In an instant, he felt pain and dropped the bug. It had bitten him. Pulling his hand to his face, he saw a tiny, bloody cut, the skin torn. When he looked down, the insects were gone, scattering into the brush. He scoured the area for them, overturning limbs and driftwood and kicking the under-brush, but to no avail. They had disappeared.

Duncan was skeptical when Boyd reported back to the office.

"You know how long a .50-caliber bullet is?" he scoffed.

"I didn't say they were the size of a .50-caliber bullet, just the shape, but they must've been eight, nine centime-ters at least," Boyd countered. "I'm tellin' you, it was big, and it bit me. Just look," Boyd held out his hand. He'd put a Band-Aid over the wound and peeled it back.

"Where?" Duncan asked. "I don't see anything."

Pulling the bandage off, Boyd waved the underside of the pad at his boss.

"See the spots of blood?"

Duncan glanced at the bandage skeptically.

"I see some blood. So you were bitten. Cockroaches can bite."

"It wasn't a cockroach. Why would I lie?" Boyd insisted. "Here, look."

He squeezed his hand where the insect had sliced him. Up popped a droplet of blood.

"Now do you believe me?"

Duncan thought the conversation was going nowhere, shrugged his shoulders and waved his hand dismissively. Changing the subject, he asked if Boyd had collected specimens.

"The specimen was the one that bit me," Boyd said

defensively. "But I've got more pictures. What you looked at were just from the first memory card. I used two."

"What's on the card?"

"I haven't looked at them yet."

Duncan held his hand out.

"Give me the card, and I'll download them into my laptop. I hope they're better shots than the first card."

Boyd grimaced. Duncan tended toward sarcasm and almost always made his criticisms known. Of course, that was part of his job with graduates. He rarely cut them slack.

Boyd fished out the camera from his bright yellow daypack and extracted the memory card.

"Now we'll see just what kind of man-eating cockroach we're dealing with," Duncan said.

Duncan wasn't certain about what he was seeing on his laptop as he returned to his desk. But he was certain it wasn't a cockroach. Boyd stood behind him, staring at the screen. It was clear to him, standing four feet from the laptop screen, that it wasn't a cockroach.

"Still think it's a cockroach?" Boyd sneered with feigned indignation.

Duncan sighed deeply as if he had been holding his breath.

"Did you get dimensions?"

"I didn't have a chance. Like I said, at least eight centimeters or more for the one that bit me, but there weren't many of them. For a few seconds, they were there and then they were gone. Didn't even have time to get the ruler out."

"There's nothing on the photos to give us scale," Duncan said.

"You know, maybe I can get it from the Exif data on the file."

"The what?"

"It's a type of file format, but it includes information about focusing, distance, et cetera."

"How does that help us?" Duncan said, looking toward Boyd.

"It should tell us the distance the lens was focusing."

Duncan looked puzzled.

"If we know how far away the object is from the lens, we might be able to make at least an educated guess about its size. I know when I grabbed it, it was longer than my hand is wide."

Duncan grabbed Boyd's left hand and slapped a plastic ruler into it.

"Let's just measure your palm," Duncan said. "Seems like that would be the easiest and maybe the most accurate way to do it."

"I guess that's why you're the boss, and I'm the worker bee."

"Not really. I've got a grant, and you don't."

The palm of Boyd's hand was almost exactly four inches wide.

"It was longer than your palm?"

"Yeah, but I can't remember by how much. It bit me almost as soon as I picked it up. It was really aggressive. It didn't try to escape until I dropped it."

"But you're sure it was bigger, so maybe we can assume it was at least four inches long."

"Yeah, sure."

"We can take that and get its width from the pictures, at least an estimate."

Using a printout, they measured the length and width of the insect. Boyd mentally calculated the thickness at one inch. They exchanged surprised looks. Duncan whistled reflexively.

"What the hell is this thing?" he wondered.

2

Fifty-four-year-old Raul Barbosa stood a chunky five-feet-four inches tall, sporting an unkempt salt-and-pepper beard that stretched nearly to his waist. It wasn't that his beard was long so much as his torso was short. His head was covered with long, thinning, mostly gray hair. He often tied it back in a ponytail. His upper lip was hidden under the thick outcropping of an untrained mustache that, when his mouth was closed, covered his lower lip. Often, when he chewed, his few remaining teeth would grab onto an unruly mustache strand and painfully pull it away from his lip. When this happened, he would use grooming scissors to cut the mustache until it no longer covered his lower lip. He was a practical man.

Barbosa came to the Rio Negro from Bogota while in his late twenties. The beetle-browed bachelor had broken up with the girl he thought would become his wife, which precipitated a weekend bender that included an assault charge alleging that he tried to strangle her in a bar, necessitating a new start out of the reach of Columbian authorities.

He had a vague plan to live off the land, but that was before he had actually tried it.

Making his living as a miner, he was both lucky and industrious. Unlike most miners he knew, he banked most of his earnings, and when he was not working retreated to the plot of land he purchased some sixty kilometers southeast of the Rio Negro town of Manaus. By the time he turned forty, he not only had learned to live in the forest but to thrive. His pride and joy was the forty-six-square-meter stilt house he'd built. The property, which stood fifty meters from a narrow creek, was accessible only by small boat. Even so, navigating from his place to the river was complicated and involved many twists and turns. It was easy to become lost and hard to find one's way. But he craved the isolation and took pride in his property, having cleared the land himself. He had help erecting the house, which cost nearly fifteen-thousand reals, including labor.

And unlike many miners who ended up dead or crippled, Barbosa had escaped his profession with only minor scrapes. His lucky break came four years ago when he won forty-thousand reals tax-free playing the Mega-Sena Lottery. That allowed him to add a solar water heater, wind turbine, and photovoltaic arrays. Although he had few friends, he kept in touch via radiotelephone with Jose Silva, who owned a small export business in Manaus. Despite having money in the bank, Barbosa was frugal, and when he wasn't tending his garden or selling his services as a fishing guide, he hunted black caiman, or *jacare*, as they are known, for meat and hides. While a black caiman purse could easily sell for six hundred American dollars, the raw hides that Barbosa sold to Silva covered his fuel cost and little more. However, he used the meat as bait to trap yellow-footed tortoises, which he sold to restaurants in Manaus for a handsome profit.

Barbosa had good luck hunting the past week, and after radioing Silva that he had several hides for him, one of them over four meters long, he began preparing to make the trip. His five-meter aluminum boat, with its fifteen-horsepower outboard, showed its age but held an affectionate place in its heart. He called it Maria and often shared his thoughts with her while on the river.

He spent an hour in the morning loading the boat. It took four trips between the cabin and the boat to finish. But he didn't work hard. He carried each hide separately and then returned to the cabin one last time for his backpack. As he dropped the shutters on the windows, he noticed something unusual in his garden. Was it locusts? Something was moving through some of the rows. Grabbing his backpack and shutting the door behind him, he descended to the ground and moved quickly to the garden. He was proud of the vegetables that he nurtured from seeds and took it personally when insects or animals, especially squirrel monkeys, attacked them. He relied on canned goods from Manaus but always looked forward to seasonal vegetables. He loved tomatoes and occasionally ate them off the vine with a pinch of freshly ground pepper.

The garden was about twenty-five meters west of the house. As he approached, he heard a soft buzzing, which grew louder with every step. Holding up at the garden's edge, he surveyed the far end, where he thought he saw movement. It occurred to him that it could be a jaguar or a snake and that his rifle and machete were in the boat. He thought about either retrieving the rifle or leaving for Manaus. But his curiosity got the best of him. He stepped into the garden cautiously, stopping halfway in to peer at the area where he'd seen the movement. The buzzing was pronounced and unlike anything he'd ever heard. At least it wasn't a snake as he'd feared. Stepping forward, he leaned toward a thick row of corn and pushed the plants to get a better view of whatever was causing the movement. He regretted it almost instantaneously.

The ground was crawling with large, cockroach-like insects. He no longer heard the buzzing. It had faded into the background like elevator music, pushed aside by the utter terror he felt as the bugs launched themselves at him, clinging to him with hatchet-like forelegs that they used to stab him over and over, drawing blood almost immediately. Dozens embedded themselves in his beard.

Barbosa stumbled backward as he wheeled on one foot but managed to keep his balance long enough to fall into several tomato cages, ending up on his hands and knees. He grabbed at the insects clinging to his shirt, but they resisted, holding fast. The ones he pulled off tore pieces out of his shirt. He could feel them hacking away on the back of his neck, his legs, and now on the top of his head. He screamed, rose to his feet, closed his eyes and lumbered forward blindly. They were attacking his eyes. He told himself to jump into the river, that immersing himself in the muddy water was his only hope. But the insects were relentless. More and more of them continued to join the attack, so much so that as he picked himself off the ground a second time he ripped two of the bugs from near his eyes, screaming with pain as chunks of his flesh went with them. He was out of the garden and could see the boat. He mouthed the words, "I have to go there," inadvertently providing the opportunity for at least one insect to scurry into his mouth and down his throat. He choked and vomited, expelling the bug. He clamped his mouth shut, but the bugs continued to attack his eyes. He screamed as they pounded away with their deadly forelegs. His vision faded quickly as the insects chopped into his cornea. Blinded, crawling in the deep grass, he no longer knew what direction he was moving. Where was the river?

"*Dio aydarme!*" he screamed, which only made things worse as several bugs entered his mouth. All he could do was dry heave as he felt them chopping away at his esophagus. If anyone had seen him from a distance, it would have looked as if he was struggling with a dark throbbing blanket.

The bugs owned Barbosa's body now. They chopped away as methodically as robots, raising tiny geysers of blood on every square inch of skin. They tunneled into his rectum and chopped away. They chopped holes in his esophagus and chopped at every organ within reach. Just as the buzzing had disappeared, the pain diminished as life leaked out of him. His body had become a sieve. And then there was a rush of blood through his anus as the bugs chopped through his rectum and into his abdomen. But it wasn't a problem for him any longer, as thousands of insects took their turn at stripping the flesh from his body.

END OF EXCERPT

Insects is now available on Amazon.

ABOUT THE AUTHOR

John Koloen, a native of Wisconsin, has been a longshore-man, construction worker, newspaperman, magazine publisher and bureaucrat. He lives in Galveston, TX, with his wife Laura.

To receive updates on John's upcoming books, please sign up for the free newsletter at watchfirepress.com/jk.

ALSO BY JOHN KOLOEN

THE INSECTS SERIES

Insects

Insects: The Hunted

Insects: Specimen

Insects: Braga's Gold

Insects: Books 1, 2 & 3

STANDALONE NOVELS

Griswold's Op

The Cabin

For more information, please visit watchfirepress.com/jk.

www.ingramcontent.com/pod-product-compliance
Lightning Source LLC
Chambersburg PA
CBHW031705170626
46808CB00005B/1618